THE CANDLEMASS ROAD

George MacDonald Fraser

THE CANDLEMASS ROAD

HARVILL
An Imprint of HarperCollins*Publishers*

First published in 1993 by Harvill
an imprint of HarperCollins*Publishers*
77–85 Fulham Palace Road,
Hammersmith, London W6 8JB

2 4 6 8 9 7 5 3 1

© George MacDonald Fraser 1993

Map drawn by Ken Lewis

The Author asserts the moral right
to be identified as the author of this work.

A CIP record for this book
is available from the British Library.

ISBN 0 00 271362 4

Photoset in Linotron Baskerville by
Rowland Phototypesetting Ltd, Bury St Edmunds, Suffolk

Printed and bound in Great Britain by
HarperCollinsManufacturing Glasgow

IN GRATEFUL MEMORY OF
JOSEPH BAIN
EDITOR OF THE CALENDAR
OF BORDER PAPERS

CONTENTS

THE CANDLEMASS ROAD

FELLOW OF CLARE HALL, being in that state where another hour's tippling should render him swine drunk, asked me, if I had a choice of all mankind that ever lived, which would I choose to sit by me as a guest at the next college feast. I made excuse that I was not of his learned society, but he said all was one for that, and I must choose or be fined in stoupes for the company. Still I would have put him off, for I longed to be quiet in my corner by the fire, away from the babble and ass-laughter of him and his companions, and have no part in their silly conceits designed to show off their wit and learning (and little they had of either) in their cups. They (and I) had been at the great masque "Ignoramus" given before his majesty, to his seeming content if not mine, but it may be that his Latin was better than I knew, or that he laughed out of courtesy, for a windier piece of dullness I never saw than that masque, that was well titled for them that applauded it, being men of the colleges. His majesty clapped patiently, so I clapped too.

It put them in a learning mood afterwards that were in the buttery, with such follies as what folk lived on the stars, and what part of the anatomy was the seat of mirth, and anon to debating what cup companion they would choose for their feast. One said Julius Caesar, and another St Francis, and others Aristotle and Ptolemy and Roger Bacon, their vanity supposing they could have held equal discourse with these champions and sages, and then seeing me that sat withdrawn, cried out that the old Portingale should speak his mind, "for he hath travelled in his time, and been a priest, too, so sure he is ignorant enough." Seeing their canary humour, I begged again to be let be.

"Nay, but ye shall answer, or be fined!" said they. "And after we'll have the breeches off thee for a sullen old rascal that hops of his left foot. Choose, now, or pay forfeit!"

Seeing no help, I said if one must sit by me at any feast of theirs, it should be Attila the Hun, so should I be spared their rudeness and intrusion. Some accounted it a good answer, and laughed, but he that had speered at me scowled and said they had none at their feasts but those they might have good of, and I must name another, since Attila was a monstrous beast that none could have any good of, being curst and altogether abominable.

At this, I, being part drunk myself, said he lied, for good might be had of the worst that ever were, in certain cases. At this he swore that if I could not prove it by logic, I should pay double forfeit and swim in the Cam for my impudence, so let me say how one could have good of Attila or any like him. His fellows grinned and gleeked about me, and some cried, "At him, old Papist!" but others "Confound the Jesuit, he mocks us, to the river with him!" and bade me make good mine argument.

First, I told them, they should name any two from whom they might hope to have the greatest good (other than Our Lord, for it was not fit to name Him in such a question). They that had named Aristotle and

2

St Francis as their chosen guests again cried out their names, and with those I was content, saying that against them I would justify Attila and another like him, as Chingis Khan or Hulagu (of whom I doubt these scholars had heard, though they cried aye to him). I would do it, I said, on an hypothesis, as thus:

"Here is any one of you, in a lonely place, as a little cabin in the wilderness, with no neighbours or friends by, and ye are sick and feeble, and with you your wife and two fair daughters."

Hereon they cried that being young they had no daughters, and would other men's daughters do, to give them solace in that lonely place, whereof they doubted not they would soon be enfeebled if not sick! I let them bray it out, and when they were quiet, continued:

"As ye lie there helpless, there approach three great thieves and murderers that ye know to be crueller than any devils, who will surely torment and slay you and ravish your wife and fair daughters, and take and burn all besides. There is no help for you at all, being at their mercy if they come in, but as ye lie in terror for what is to come, a knock falls on the nether door of your poor cabin, as it may be some wayfarer seeking lodging or refreshment. Aye, and it may be he will lend you aid against your enemies approaching! You bid your wife open in haste. Now tell me, scholars, what men do you hope to see there when she opens? The learned, gentle Aristotle and St Francis the meek, or Attila the great Hun armed cap-a-pie with Chingis at his elbow? From which pair, in your sore need, shall you hope to have the greater good, the saintly philosophers or the lusty men of war?"

They cried out with scorn that between the enemies

before and Attila at their back, it was all one, they should have nothing but evil at the hands of either.

"Not so," says I, and bade them look in the chronicles, "for there you shall read that the Scythian and the Mungul both, though in their conquests they were monsters of cruelty that put whole nations to the sword, yet in their private and domestic ways were zealous for good order and discipline of law, being such as would not suffer weak or poor folk to be despoiled or hurt by thieves and ravishers. Aye, of that Chingis was it said that while he carpeted all Asia with bones, yet might a virgin with a bag of gold walk the length of his dominions without harm, so perfect was his governance. So, again I say, who shall better serve you in time of peril, the philosophers who wish you well but cannot front the murderers save with words, or the bloody ravagers of empires who are yet ready to turn their weapons against common spoilers?"

At this they fell to babbling and dispute, and one fell down drunk crying "Paradox! Paradox!" while another said that for all he knew Aristotle might be a right swashing boy when it came to a fray. I asked would he wager on him with sword and buckler against my two savages, let roaring Francis give what aid he might, and he said, no, not at any odds. And while a few of them held that such as Attila and Chingis would do no good service to any, the more held that I had made my case, and should not be fined or insulted, but pressed more drink upon me that I durst not refuse for fear of their rough merriment, and called me a jolly old Pope, and how I came home I know not, for they found me sodden among the cabbages in the almshouse garden, and I was two weeks abed thereafter with the sciatica.

4

And lying there, and not able to read more than a little for the infirmity of mine eyes that are worn with looking on the world's wickedness four score years, I fell to meditating on the good that evil men may do, by design or more commonly by chance, and was vexed that I had not told the Clare fellows how this same Attila, through his ravaging of Lombardy, had caused the folk to flee to those lagoons where they made the town of Venice, which is now surely a great state that hath given much of commerce and art to mankind, and all because of Attila his wickedness! Which I doubt not would have confused their debate that was confused enough already with their bowsing. Howbeit, I say, I thought on the good of evildoers, and concluded to my satisfaction that it is not one-thousandth of the evil that good and wise men do with their blundering, well as they intend.

Thinking on this wise, and looking to mine own past, I remembered sundry instances that I had seen, and in especial the man Waitabout, that I knew only for a little season, yet it changed my life's course, and indeed had been like to lose my poor life for me, yet was I spared, "by God's grace", a phrase I speak now but by habit and long use, for if He hath any grace (or indeed any being at all save in men's minds only) I have long been removed from it. Which is a blasphemy, as they say, yet I have known worse. No, I am no priest, nor ever was except to the outer eye, for what priest ever doubted, and with long doubting, gave over his belief at last?

As to the Waitabout, he was no Attila yet had done ill enough in his time, and if he did good it was upon compulsion and for a brief hour only, and still I know not whether it was good or no. But certain it is he was no common man, though common seeming, a robber and slayer and broken wanderer that had in him, I think, the making of a sage if not a saint. He read me a lesson, aye, and so too did my Lady Dacre, though what it was I can hardly tell even now. Yet I would tell of them both that have been out of my mind these many years, saving that visit my lady paid me five years agone, fair and smiling still and brought me a gift of candles of fine Italian wax, though not scented, "for we shall burn no incense between us, nor make graven images neither," as she said, which was an old jest between us. "A remembrance of Candlemass," says she, "aye, of the Candlemass road," and told me they had made a ballad of it, and of what befell betwixt the fires at Triermain, which I marvelled to hear her speak of so lightly. But of Waitabout she spake not at all.

If I am to tell of that road, I cannot come to it direct, for that would be to begin *in medias res*, as we clerks say when we mean in the midst of things but wish to awe the commonalty with our learning (give us a fourth tassel, good Lord, for vanity!), but must needs give some preamble, about myself, and then come in proper order to Waitabout, or Archie Noble as his name was, called Lang Archie, or Wait-about-him, or Master Noble as my lady styled him once or twice, I think to his content, for broken men are not used to such courtesies. Of myself first then, not out of pride, but for your better understanding of that which follows. And it is right, too, that the gown should take precedence of the *renegado*.

I, Luis Guevara, once a priest and ever a sinner, was born in Portugal, and came to England by a long road which it would weary you as much to hear as me to travel. It took me to the Americas, and the coasts of Barbary and Africa, in the service of God, and at last to

London, no matter why, in the twenty-fourth year of the old Queen's reign, where chance took me in the way of Ralph, Lord Dacre. We were as little like as could be, he the great noble, favoured of the Queen, with the honours of soldiery upon him and all trappings of wealth and power, which he carried like a conqueror, for he was a terrible man – and I, the little foreign priest that feared for my very life in a land where priests were welcome as the plague. It was the time of the great bill against the Jesuits, when to be a Roman priest was treason, and the harbouring of us a felony; there were many then burned for the Faith.

"A poor candle you would make," says my lord. "Why, man, ye would not light me up the stair!" And laughed at me, a great bull of a man as he was, all in crimson save for the blue charge upon his breast that bare a bull indeed, the red bull of his house, and stood on legs like tree trunks, grinning from a face great as a ham, bald of crown with white hair to his shoulders. "Aye, we are tonsured, the two of us, but you can say Mass and I cannot nor would not, but since the half of my folk are recusant and will not be turned, needs must I a priest, go to!"

I told him it was treason, and that if he sheltered me, let alone gave employ, he would be liable before the law.

"The law! Pish on the law!" and put his head on one side. "Have ye heard o' the Leges Marchiarum, priest – the Law of the Marches? No? It is the only law in my whereabouts, and says naught of religion. Let be, I make my own law, and if I take the Pope himself into my house to minister to my silly poor folk, not the Queen's Grace herself shall say cheep! No, nor all the bishops. For I am Dacre. Will fifty shillings a year content you?"

I trembled to hear him, but asked sixty shillings and a chapel decently kept, whereon he laughed till he shook and said I should have them for my boldness. And gripped my hand in a hard clasp, looking narrowly on me, and said we would do well together being of a middle age and not loth to speak our minds one to the other, "but not of your old faith, for I'll none of it. Keep it for my vassals." Which I did and have ever done, without fear of the law, for all that he said was true. He had done such service against Scotch invaders and English rebels, and was in such fair regard of my Lord Burleigh and the Queen, who called him "cousin Dacre" and "my red steer", there being some kinship through the Grays, I believe, that he might do as he pleased in his barony far off on the border. They had need of him yonder, and my Lord Cecil was wont to jest on the words of the King of France, that the Scotch frontier was worth a Mass so it was said quietly.

My Lord Ralph was down to London only to put his grandchild into the Court as ward of Her Grace. I saw the little maid but once, a sweet pretty child of four years, proper and toward and well grown, straight in her petty gown and proud of her kerchief of French point. "See my kercher," says she. "'Tis white, and I keep it clean. You are my grandad's Italian man, but you must not sing at me." To her all Romans were Italians. She passed by with her head in air, playing with her kerchief.

So my lord went north to his estate in Cumberland hard by the border line, taking in his train his "Portingale preacher", as he pleased to call me.

Now I have been about the world, as I said, and travelled far for the Faith in my nonage and after. I was with those Spaniards who sought the Strait of Anian which men say lies beyond the Americas, and suffered ship-wreck on that arid coast beneath Guaymas where I was captive of the wild Indians. I have been among their savage brethren of Mexico, and undergone the torments with which they afflict their prisoners before the great step-temples of the forest which rise higher than Salis-bury spire, and so far forgot my vows to take part against them when Mendoza the Good defended the silver mines on the Compostela road. I have journeyed in the black lands of Lower Africa where the people cut their faces for adornment, and make sacrifice of their enemies and eat their flesh for meat. And for a time I was a slave of the Algerines, and saw such horrors as would blast the sight, of men impaled and torn asunder and flung upon great hooks. All this I have seen among the heathen, but I have yet to see such savages as were in the Marches of England and Scotland when first I went there with my Lord Dacre.

You may think I have an old man's memories that swell up with age, but you do not know, you who live in this green quiet country with its fair pleasaunces by the Cam, and the little towns and hamlets where they cry alarm if a deer is potched or a schoolboy robs an orchard. You may journey now, from York to the Kingdom of Fife, through what you have been taught to call the Middle Shires, and meet with nothing more fierce than a beggar crying for alms by the roadside. You forget, if you ever knew, that a bare five and twenty years since there were three realms in this country that we call Great Britain: there was England and Scotland – and the Borderland between. Two realms at peace, civil and quiet under their native laws, with good governance from London and Edinborough, the folk giving glad allegiance

(for the most part) to royal Elizabeth and royal James –
and where they joined, a land neglected and cursed,
peopled by two-legged beasts who lived by robbery and
feud and murder and terror, a country where reprisal
followed raid by the clock, where every nightfall brought
its toll of men butchered and dwellings burned and cattle
reft and hostages carried away. It was spoil, spoil, spoil,
from Tweed mouth to Sark; never a moment but there
were thieves in the saddle, Scot against Englishman,
Englishman against Scot, and both together against each
and every, and no peace any way. I have gone a-horse-
back one day east from Carlisle town, and seen thirty
churches in ruin, and great abbeys tumbled down on the
Scotch side, and the conies running through what had
been fair hamlets a week before, and now all black and
smoking, and bodies unburied on every hand, and
women and babes wandering in the desolation.

And this was no war. It was, they said, the custom of
the country, and no help for it. The laws of England
and Scotland were clean withdrawn, and only the Leges
Marchiarum, of which my lord spoke, that Border law,
under which a great thief might compound for the most
horrid crime with a fine and interest, and assurance of
good behaviour, but no other punishment – and so to
the next riding and slaughter. And this in Christendom,
only a score of years ago.

When first I went there, I was told of a traveller who
had inquired of the people, where the Christians dwelt,
to which they made answer, "No Christians, sir, we are
Elliots and Armstrongs." I thought it a blasphemous
jest, but it was true. God had forgotten the Borderland,
or turned away from its wickedness in His despair.

You may wonder why my Lord Dacre, who had fair

lands in the far south, such as this where I live out the winter of my time, should keep his home in such a den of strife and iniquity. But he was one who craved a hard life, and must be doing; it was in him to dare, and if there had been no Cumberland I believe he would have made his bed in Tartary. Moreover, his house had held their own on that stark border three hundred years, through the bitter Scotch wars in which the people of the Marches had their tempering – and this, I am assured, was why they must continue to live like warring nomads, for it was bred in their nature. He would not shrink from it, not for all the gold and quiet of the south country, which he might have had in plenty. "For I am Dacre," he would say. "Shift me an ye can."

It was as though the fiend had taken him at his word, for his estate of Askerton lay in the worst part of all the border, where the baddest of the thieves were wont to run their roads – for so they called their forays, raid and road being all one to them; in the same sort they called their going forth in any number a "gang". He had broad acres, and many fat cattle, and fifteen score tenants in petty villages and farms about, all in that pretty land that lies fifteen miles or so north and east of Carlisle, where the rich champain ground runs to the foot of the fells. So close to Carlisle, the strongest hold in all the Marches, and the seat of what government there was on the English side, should have been safe enough, but it was not so. To the east lay the great Waste, the highway of the robbers, and beyond, Tynedale, a great haunt of English thieves, Charltons and Milburns and Robsons and the like, for they robbed as families, calling them-selves "riding surnames". To the west was the country of the Grahams, a barbarous nation, Scotch or English for all that any man knew, but mostly English. There too was the Debatable Land, that had been of neither country, and only lately divided between them jealously, and a great nest of outlaws. Yet to the north was worst of all, a scant ten miles away, for there on the very rim of the frontier lay the valleys of the most feared Scotch robbers, the Nixons and Armstrongs and Crosiers and Elliots, who dwelt in Liddesdale, and if there be a Hell, and it hath a mouth, then it gapes at the foot of that dark and terrible glen, and those within are devils incarnate.

When a man has such neighbours he goes to bed late and lies not long in the morning, but my lord throve on it as it were sport. And being an expert borderer and skilly soldier, he gave so much better than he took that in his last years we began to have some quiet in the lands about Askerton, though the rest of the frontier corrupted by the day. Even the hardiest freebooters, Armstrongs of Mangerton and Whithaugh, Elliots of Stobs and the Park, and Grahams of Brackenhill and Eden, began to look for their living otherwise than on Dacre's ground, and rode wide of the Red Bull's pen. It was a grisly A.B.C. that he learned them. I have seen his great gallows beyond the barnekin, four ells high and four across the beam, loaded with such a cargo of dead thieves as would have gorged me every crow from Kelso to Caldbeck, and not a day but there was fresh fodder for them, swinging in the cold fell wind.

And if the meanest of his tenants was spoiled of so much as a hen, then out from Askerton's gate would come the red steer banner, and my lord in his silver-studded jack, lance on thigh, and his grey locks streaming in the wind, and at his back fifty, aye, or a hundred riders, every man in his steel cap with sword or Jedburgh axe, and the turf of hot trod smoking on his esquire's point. They would ride Liddesdale to Riccarton and back, to Smailholm Tower or the Rede banks, leaving red ruin behind them, and there would be widows crying in Teviotdale for their men on the Askerton gallows. And when those he had despoiled and punished cried to the Wardens to summons him to answer at the next truce day, he would give the officer who brought the bill such entertainment as would have contented an ambassador, and when he had eaten and drunk his fill Ralph Dacre would press the bill back in his hand, wrapped in a glove, and say:

"Bid Lord Scroop at Carlisle (or Carmichael at Dumfries, or the Keepers of Liddesdale or Tynedale, as it might be) good cheer, and tell them they may foul their bill against me, and who will collect their double and sawfey?" Which is to say, the threefold penalty of restitution imposed on one found guilty of offence. "I ride against none, nor never did, that has done me no hurt. Let the Wardens keep their border – but not 'twixt Hethersgill and Triermain, for that is my charge, and mine alone."

And the Wardens, who had grief enough, were glad to let his bill be continued, or adjourned. They were driven lords, with not money nor equipment nor men enough to do any good in all that frontier of decay; they were content that one so rich and strong, that had the Queen's ear, should stand as a rock of order in a sea of misrule.

You would suppose, in such a parish, that I was seldom idle, but for the most I was occupied with my lord's tenants, the simple folk of the estate who clung to the faith of their fathers. They were few enough, the others

13

taking their lead in the new religion from their lord, and in his household I was forbidden to meddle.

So for seventeen years I dwelt in Askerton Hall, doing my duty with a failing heart, for I saw nothing but the wickedness of the world about me, and knowing a dripping on my soul that wears away faith, more even than I had known in the pagan places. I was weary with the weight of evil and my more than three score years, but without the will to go elsewhere.

Then on a summer's day my lord took him to the races at Carlisle, where one of his troopers won the Bell on my lord's grey, Sandeman, wherefore he was in great fettle, as they say here, and gave entertainment at the Apple Tree on the Drover's Lane to my lords Scroop, and Willoughby of the East March, and that good man Carmichael, and others less good, such as Hutcheon Graham the brigand, and Kerr of Cessford that they called "Fyrebrande", and the young Buccleuch who had broken open Carlisle Castle but three years before – for the strangeness of these people is how they make company together, the lord and the peasant, the Scotch thief and the English constable, men that were at handstrokes o' Thursday drinking together on the Saturday. I have seen that Kinmont Will, the bloodiest rogue on the West border, cheek by jowl with my Lord Hunsdon, who held the English Mid-March as the Queen's Warden, as they made wagers on Hunsdon's son, young Robin Carey who was his father's deputy, when he played at football on the Bitts, whether he would win one goal or two. The thief and the catcher at game together, content each in company of the other. But it is their way, unless feud should fall between them, which it may as easily for a broken cup as for a broken head, and yet they forgive each other grievous wrongs, too. But deadly feud they pursue to the death, not only of the enemy but of all his kinsfolk. They take joy of their difference from mankind, Scot and English together, for though they are of both realms, they are first and last of the Border.

But I wander, in my dotage. My Lord Ralph won the Bell, and parted in the evening from his foe-friends, and rode out by the Rickergate with two grooms for company, to fare home to Askerton. They were waiting for him on the Brampton road, men in visors, well-horsed, and they shot him through with calivers, nine balls in his body, and he let die by the roadside. They killed the grooms with their swords, and made away. Who they were was not found out. Some suspected Hutcheon Graham, but he made oath on his father's stone in St Cuthbert's churchyard of Carlisle, so he was clean, and I believe it, for in all my time yonder I never knew a word broken, for all their other faults. Sundry were named, Lance Carleton and Black Ogle and Stark Jack Charlton of Tynedale on the English side, and on the Scottish, Will Kang, that was a notable murderer for hire, and the Scotts of Teviotdale, and as for the Liddesdales, why, who you will. The truth was, my lord had more ill-willers than hairs on his head; he was a terrible man, but a good friend to me-ward, and while he lived his folk slept secure, and his cattle grazed untroubled even on the lion's lip.

He was buried at Arthuret, before a great company, and my lord Bishop himself came from Carlisle to say his solemns, with staff and mitre and many attendants and a singing choir within. There were many lords there, and I marvelled to see so many notable thieves there also, of both sides. Some said, in scandalous jest, that

15

they came to see him well delved under, but I think otherwise, for I have seen that affinity that grows betwixt enemies, who while they hate lustily in life, yet sorrow when death parts them. They are a strange folk. I heard one say, "Now he is at peace," and another made answer saying he wished his soul no peace, but great action wheresoever it had gone, for that he had loved above all. My lords Scroop and Willoughby and the Scots Warden Carmichael bore his bier, and among the others that Scott of Harden whom they called Auld Wat, a principal reiver, and the young Buccleuch and John Carey, who were no friends to each other elsewhere.

In all this I had no part, being what they styled a recusant, but came hooded and cloaked to give no offence, which they overlooked, knowing well what I was. I gave back, thinking I had never seen so much costly stuff and apparel mingled with such a deal of leather and steel by a graveside, and as I stood at the church door I saw that which lessoned me even more what a contrary country is this, for as the Lord Bishop led them in prayers, all standing sodden in the rain, there in the church porch sat Long Tom Hetherington, a great villain that they called "the Merchant", casting the accounts of blackmail that he and his fellow-robber Richie Graham had wrung from the poor folk thereabouts. Now this blackmail, or black rent, is an extortion much practised by the thieves, who come to a man, or a village, and say, pay us such-and-such and you and your possessions will be safe, for we shall see to it, but if ye pay not, look to it, for sundry reivers will doubtless ride upon you (by which they mean their wicked selves). And the poor folk are wont to pay to be left in peace. It is a protection money and one of the principal curses of the frontier in those days. Because of my old lord's zeal and care of his people, none on Dacre ground had paid this black rent to any for a half-score years, but this was in Arthuret that lay beyond our bounds. Yet it took me by the throat to see this vile money-changer at his practices in the House of God, and my lord not cold in the ground.

"Have ye no shame," I asked him, "that ye count your blood money in the church, and the bell yet tolling for the dead?"

He looked at me astonied, saying there was none of Dacre's folk on his books "and where else should I keep them for safety but in the kirk where the clients come to pay, and this the day? Would ye have us run about the country, chapping at gates, for our black rent?"

I could have struck him, for all he had his sword naked by his books, but it was no place or time and I a priest. "Keep them in your thieves' den at Brackenhill Tower, with your vile confederate Richie Graham," I bade him, and he laughed.

"Thinkst thou I'd trust them within Richie's reach? Go to, man, y'are wandered! Get thysel' back to Askerton, confess thy young maids, and I'll help thee penance them!"

And sat there taking his extortion, which is crime the world over, but here it was open, and the lords at the grave and the Warden officers and constables marked him not, for that it was but lightly regarded and, as they say, the custom of the country!

Now I see that the preambulation to my tale has taken longer than I would it had, yet my excuse is that I had need tell you of my poor self and my old lord, and of my being at Askerton, and not only that but to lay open to you the ways of the frontier and the godless folk therein, at some length, with illustration of their manners, that you may understand perfectly all that befell on that Candlemass that I spoke of, which I shall now come to before long, I do assure you.

It was in the summer time that my lord departed this life, and all through the back end and winter unto the February following we that had served him lived a-tiptoe in Askerton Hall, wondering when the thieves would ride on our goodly land and livestock, now that the Red Bull was no more. For his armed following were all dispersed to seek other employs, having no mind to bide at Askerton without him to lead them, and we were but a household reduced, the bailiff and myself and the servitors, with no security for the tenants and farms. Yet they rode not against us that winter, such was the shadow of his name, and also because in the cold months the herds were away at softer pasturing in the deep vales by the lakes, in which hard time the riding surnames were wont to rest them in their towers and bastels, and the outlaws in the mosses. Yet was there rumour that with the mastiff dead the foxes soon would prowl, and word of Liddesdale spears spying below the Lyne rivers against the coming of spring, when the great thieves would burst forth of their lairs and, in their barbarous phrase, shake loose the border.

So were we in apprehension, but took comfort from word that had reached us at Christmas, that my Lady Dacre that was grand-daughter to old Lord Ralph as I told you I met her when a little maid, was to come up into the country from London, she being his only kin and heiress to all his great wealth and estates. Whereof we were right glad, for we doubted not that her advisers would take order for the security of the Askerton demesne. Indeed I wondered that she should come in her own person, being but a young woman and long away from that fierce country, when her men of affairs could have been sent, and she continued in her enjoyment of southern pleasantry. But it hath been whispered in mine ear since, that the Queen herself willed it so, for a reason, to wit, that my Lady Margaret having been in waiting on the Queen, had given her offence by her temper, which was as proud, and her stomach as high, as even Her Grace's, and that was not small, God knows.

Also there had been talk of my Lady Margaret's commerce with certain young lords at the Court having given displeasure to Her Grace, for she was none of your lily maids, but free and frank in her manner, as I had seen when she was little, and I doubt not she smiled whither she pleased, caring not if it misliked Her Grace or no. This may be scandal of the sort they love to tattle after in London, but the long and short was that the Queen commanded her away. So we had great heave and ho at Askerton against her coming, and myself much perturbed, wondering would she tolerate me, the Portingale priest, as her grandsire had done, he being careless in such matters, as I have shown, but she, coming from the Court, it was not to be doubted that she was strong for the reformed church, and like to turn me away, or worse. And at my time of life I knew not whither to go if she dismissed me.

Candlemass was the day pricked for her coming in, and though we knew it not, it was to be the day of Archie Noble Waitabout's coming also. She was looked for by open day, but he that was not looked for came like a thief in the night while the house slept, and none sounder than I.

19

EING THEN IN that state of years when the aches of my limbs and back cured not with resting, and the great scaur on my leg that I had of the Mexican savages troubling most of all, sleep was a sweet relief, and I was wont to drowse abed in the mornings, like any sluggard, but comfortable. None in that household seeking my offices, I had fallen into neglect of all duty, and was seldom abroad before prime. But that Candlemass I was afoot early, it being the day of my lady's coming in, and we having word that she had lain the night at Naworth, only a short way off, which, thinks I, will have done little for her temper. It had been a fair priory before the old King worked his will on such places, but fallen into neglect lately, and little apt to furnish entertainment for gentle folk. I trembled, too, for our condition at Askerton, for old Lord Ralph had lived somewhat rough, and neglected the comforts of the house, which had not bettered since his death, and was, to tell truth, sadly decayed, for the slatterns swept it but idly, and nothing was clean.

I had remonstrated with Master Hodgson, who was the bailiff, but had no satisfaction there. He was an honest man enough, stout and hearty, but of that choleric temper which makes for tyranny in one when he is given

rule over others and hath himself no very quick understanding. A good and honest steward to my lord, knowing then his duties within their limits, but now all the
care and management was on him, and it was beyond
him, so that he made great stir and noise among the
tenants, bidding them this and that, but all to no purpose, and for the household he never ceased to complain
and carp, with "Godamercy, the fire's out!" and "Where
the devil are those lackbrain men got to?", and swearing
he must do all himself – but nothing ever done. He was
in a great taking for my lady's arrival, sending the boys
up the hill to spy her carriage, and hindering the wenches
with his bustling and roaring in the kitchen, and fearful,
I think, for his shortcomings over the estate, with rents
not properly reckoned or accounts made, for he wrote
but poorly, and for figuring commend me to the village
dunce. I had offered my help, but he waved me away,
saying affairs were not for priests, and more ink on his
elbows than on the page. Yet he was an honest man, and
meant well, but without my old lord to direct him he
was adrift in confusion.

Thinking it well that some things at least should be in
order for my lady, I bade the wenches scour and polish
in my lord's old bedroom, and put out the best linen,
with lavender between the sheets, and make all as pretty
as might be, and myself set to with broom and dusters
in the hall, so that there should be one chamber fit for
her reception. I raised dust enough for a mill, and with
the help of the kitchen loon, Wattie, a great lubber that
could have stood billy to Callaban in the play, made shift
to remove all the holly and bay and rosemary hung for
Christmas, Candlemass being the time when it is taken
down. I would have had it away and burned before, but

Master Hodgson nayed me, saying it must wait for the day, as in my lord's time.

We made what order we could in the hall, with fresh rushes and green stuff in a pot, and took away the mould-iest of the tapestry, but we could no way hide the cracked leather of the chairs, or the scaurs on the table, or the moth in the bit carpet that covered it, or the sad neglect of the walls where the damp had come in. Wattie put wood on the great fire, but it was green and bubbled and stank with smoke like the pit, which was of a piece, for he fouled more than he cleaned. Welcome home, my lady, thinks I, to this draughty dirty barn, to the wind and the rain and the bare hillside and the company of animals and Cumbrians, and if ye tarry longer than to change your shoon and rest your cotchman, I shall be the more amazed.

I said as much, comparing our appointments with that she had known at Court, and was rebuked for my pains by the lurden Wat (for there is no respect in these people), who doubted not she would take joy to be home again, and find all to her liking. I took leave to doubt it, and was told, with a great sniff of his scabby nose, and sidelong nods, that I did not know her.

"And you do, to be sure," said I, and was taken at my word.

"I did," says he, grown solemn, "when she was a little bit lass, afore she went doon tae London, alack the day! I was in't stable then – aye, I put her on her first pony. Little Lady Madge, we ca'd her, and she ca'd me Wattie boy, that she did. 'Help us up, clumsy Wat!' Hey, hey, a grand wee lass! I mind when she fell in't Ghyll Beck and cam' hame blubberin' wi' a girt scratch on her arm, and I lapped it wi' a clout and dried her eyes and took

22

her to't buttery, and old Granny Sowerby gi'd her dandelion and burdock, and the la'l soul supped it and cried for mair. Hey, hey, a grand wee lass!"

It moved me to see this churl so devoted, and I asked him, would she still be the same little lass, seventeen long years after? Time, I told him, might have wrought a change.

"Never!" cries he. "She's a Dacre, aye, and a Cumberland lass, ever and a'!"

I told him she had been maid in waiting on the Queen's Grace, "and it may be that she no longer falls in streams or drinks dandelion. Your little playmate will be a great lady now, Master Wat."

"She was a great leddy when she was four year old and put vinegar in her grandad's beer," says he, with a great laugh. "Aye, and 'Whee's pissed in this pot?' cries my old lord. And the wee lass supped her milk and cries: 'And whee's pissed in this pot, an' a'?' Hey, but my lord laughed till he cried! Aye, aye, a grand la'l lass!"

I saw there was no waking him from his dream of bygone, and bade him mend the fire with dry logs from the cellar, but at this he made three great O's with his eyes and mouth and swore he could not go to the cellar without the bailiff's leave, "for they have the broken man bound there".

I asked him, what broken man, and he said, why, the vagrant fellow Archie Waitabout, that had been taken in the hind-night pilfering from the kitchen of bread and cheese, and the grooms waking had seized and bound him and cast him in the cellar at the bailiff's bidding.

So now I am come at last to Archie Noble Wait-about-him, for this was the first I ever heard of him, and little enough it seemed but a petty filching matter. I asked what they would do with him, and Wattie said they would hold him for the Warden's men, who should take him to Carlisle, there to be hung up for a broken man and thief.

"What, for bread and cheese?" said I, and Wattie said for that and other things, for it seemed he was well-known thereabouts (though not to me) for a wandering, lifting rascal of the sort that is ever under suspicion. I would have made naught of this, but for a phrase that the loon Wattie dropped among his babbling.

"Master Hodgson calls him a drawlatch and a gallow-clapper and I know not what," says he. "Aye, and a great talker, seest thou, father, so Master Hodgson says let him chatter his Latin to the Warden's men and see how it shall serve him."

Now at this my curiosity was on edge, that had thought little before, for you must know that a broken man is beneath all others mean in the borderland, the term "broken" signifying one that hath no loyalty or allegiance to any lord or leader, as most men do, but is an outcast, of the sort that are wont to band themselves together as outlaws, or, as seemed with this Waitabout, do wander solitary getting what they can. That such should break into our kitchen to steal was no wonder, but if, as Wattie said, he had Latin, then it was a portent, for I should as soon look for learning in a Barbary ape. Wherefore I inquired closely of Wattie what manner of man was this Archie Waitabout, and learned enough for my pains, for Wat was one that would sooner talk than drink so it kept him from his work.

Thus, he told me, this Waitabout was ever on the edge of all mischiefs, and had been whipped the length of the

Marches for little offences, and lain in Haddock's Hole that is a verminous prison to Berwick, and was dross to honest folk. And yet, said my Wattie, warming to his tale, it was said that in his time he had been an approved man, and done good service to my lord Hunsdon in the War of the Bankrupt Earls, and fought stoutly for the Laird Johnstone in the Lockerbie battle with the Maxwells, yet had declined in fame and fortune, no man knew how, till now he was of no account and broken, scratching for a living as he could, and thieving out of our larder in the night.

"They say he was a clerk, an' a', an' reads an' writes, but I know nowt o' that," says Wattie, all a-grin. "He's a daft 'un, I reckon, but Master Hodgson says they'll hang him for the horse."

I asked, what horse, and learned that they had come on a pretty mare out by the barnekin that dawn, and this the beast on which Waitabout had come to our kitchen door, "and a bonny hobby it is, father, wi' Spanish leather an' silver snaffle, as I saw meself. Master Hodgson reckons trash like Archie Noble never came honest by sic a mount as yon. 'The Warden's men can speer what gentleman's left his stable-door off the sneck lately,' says he, 'and then, goodnight, Archie Waitabout!'"

To this simpleton it seemed a great jest that a broken man should hang, and indeed it was nothing out of the common, save that this was a broken man with a difference, by his account, if indeed what he prattled was true, which I something doubted. Howbeit, on Master Hodgson's coming in and sending Wattie, with cuffs and curses, about some errand, I asked him if it was true that this Waitabout should to Carlisle to be hanged on suspicion of a horse, and if so I might do him some good by my office.

At this he flew into a taking, begging me plague him not about a petty villain that was naught and would soon be less. He had, he vowed, more to think on than a mere sneak-bait, aye, marry, had he! He paced about the hall, snapping his fingers and his great red face a-shake, like one beset with care and doubt that he wills not to speak of, lest it sound worse in the telling and so frights him the more. I asked him what was the matter, and he scratched his head and rolled his eyes, and at last made answer with that which put all thought of Waitabout clean out of my head.

But an hour since, that very morning, had come to him one George Bell of Triermain, a village at the easter end of my lord's land, with his head broke and his shirt bloody and a great tale of woe how five stout men of the Nixons, Scotch thieves of Liddesdale, had come to his place in the night and beaten him full sore because, they said, he had not paid his blackmail. They had made free of his house and meat and ale, put all his folk of Triermain in fear, and vowed if they were not paid to come the next night and do worse.

"Blackmail? How can that be?" I asked him, for as I told you it was a thing unheard of these many years on Dacre land, so perfect had been my lord's care of his folk. Hodgson answered me with oaths that Bell had confessed to paying the Nixons in years past, but secretly for dread of my lord's anger "who had he known would ha' whipped Bell's arse frae here to Hexham, aye, and run the Nixons ragged too!" Then for a season the Nixons had let him alone, doubtless for fear my lord should get wind of their extortion, but now, my lord being dead, they made bold to revive it, "and when Bell crieth that he hath not money to pay lawful white rent to the Dacres and black rent to Liddesdale – a thing he did privily for years, God kens! – the Nixons rattle his head to learn him better and swear to burn his thatches and carry his beasts and himself into Scotland! And Bell, sheep that he is, comes whining to me for protection!" He stamped and was like to tear his hair in vexation. "Here's grand news for my lady when she comes in! And who'll she blame for it? Her poor bailiff, owd Robby Hodgson!"

I asked him how he had answered Bell, and what was to be done for him.

"I bade him seek the Land Sergeant at Gilsland. 'What,' says he, 'go to Tom Carleton that's in the pocket of every reiver of England and Scotland both? I'll no justice of him!' I asked him what then, and the lousy sneakbill says he'll bear plaint to my lady when she comes in, for that she is his landlord now, and bound to keep him safe!" On this he was at a loss to speak further, grinding his teeth, and when I asked how he had answered said he had put his boot to Bell's backside and sent him packing.

"And yet," says he, all chapfallen, "I fear me he will find occasion to clatter at my lady's ear, and mow and girn for his cracked pate to move her pity – and seest thou, father, it will look ill for me, a tenant oppressed crying Justice! and I can do nowt for him, wanting power at hand, and but the bailiff." He called Bell an earwig and a bastard and worse, that had not the wit to pay his blackmail as in the past, so all would have been quiet.

It seemed to me he was more greatly wroth against the victim than the thief, and more sorry for himself than for the harried tenants. Here you see the cancer of the

frontier at work, a poor soul put to extortion, and his
superior, for peace and appearance, would have him pay
the blackmail, for all that it is a crime to pay as to take.
This winking at evil, for convenience, is the root of half
the mischief of the world, yet men will always wish to
be quiet.

My heart was sore for that poor lady soon to come in
to this world of bloody faction and decay, from a Queen's
Court where they played and sang and made their petty
intrigues on what young lord smiled on what young lady,
and cried Oh! if Her Majesty frowned. That is the worst
she knows, thinks I, and how shall she believe that such
folk as the Nixons can be?

Hodgson doubted but she would find out fast enough,
and fell to bewailing my lord his death, in whose time the
thieves dare not say Bo! to Askerton. "For this attempt of
the Nixons is but a pinprick!" cries he and trembled.
"Let it go unanswered we shall have such roads ridden
upon us, what of Liddesdale, what of Tynedale, what of
the broken bands, as we have not seen this ten year. The
thieves will bristle up and spur! I know it, I know them!"

When I said this was for the future, and the Wardens
should take order to prevent it, he turned on me nigh
weeping.

"Aye, but who shall answer the Nixons now, this very
night, when they ride on Triermain? Not Tommy Carleton, nor his jack-snippet deputy, nor yet Jack Musgrave
that's captain o' Bewcastle Fort and has lain swine drunk
since Martinmass and stirreth not from his bed but for
another flask and so back to his strumpet! For truth it
is as Bell says that they have policy with the thieves and
would not offend them for such a trifle."

I rebuked him that the officers named were duty bound

28

to see Bell secure, and he gave a great crack of his thumb in my face for scorn, and brayed that they would make excuse that Askerton was beyond their charge, and since my old lord had made it all his own business, so Askerton must answer Askerton's foes.

"So who must guard Triermain? The landlord! What's he? A slip of a lass, go to! And if the thieves ride in earnest, where will her tenants be and her rents withal?" He fell to damning Bell most grossly that was the cause of it all, to his mind, for not paying his black rent. And finding no remedy in raving turned his wrath on the lout Wattie, crying that the fire was out and my lady expected hourly.

Myself kept counsel, yet did share his fears that if this attempt of the Nixons in a little matter was not met, other evildoers would take example, and Askerton ridden to ruin. And as I paced about the withery orchard thinking we had been so tranquil, and now all upside down, what of thieves riding and a loose fellow in the cellar and my lady to come in, poor soul, that I was troubled for, in to me comes that same Thomas Carleton, Land Sergeant of Gilsland (which is a potent office, like to a petty Warden), and his deputy Yarrow, that had ridden over from Gilsland to give welcome to my lady, as befitted them. This Carleton was a tall smooth man with a sheep's face, easy and affable enough but cold in the eye, reckoned an expert borderer that knew the hinder-end of all things and how the world wagged, a stout man at war but a politician foremost, that for all his assurance I would have trusted no farther than I might throw Hermitage Keep. He passed for gentry, being of a known family, and discoursed with the nobility or cracked with the commonalty. His underling Yarrow was a border

29

callant with a noisy laugh and an empty head, yet proper in his gait and a fine figure, with much sense of his little office.

"God send you find the cares of the Church less than I find those of the state, sir priest," was the Land Sergeant's greeting to me, whereon I told him that if my cares were less than his, still mine lasted longer, going beyond the grave, to which he answered pleasantly that if I pursued my duties so far I would have hot work of it. So having stropped his wit, he inquired when my lady was expected. "An occasion," says he, "for 'tis not every day a Dacre comes home."

At which Master Hodgson coming out to us said he minded those that had come home other wise, slung like a peddlar's pack over a saddle-bow, and stiffer than January washing, aye, and with a hole in them made by the Land Sergeant himself, and winked at me.

"Unseasonable chat," says Carleton. "Times change, and if every family that I have touched with a sword were still mine enemies, I'd have few friends to count. In the way of business I let daylight in and blood out of Crookback Leonard Dacre in years past, and the land was the better for it. But that's by-with. Ralph Dacre was a worthy man, we sorted well, and it befits that I give handsel to his grand-daughter, as officer and friend, offering what service I may."

I said this was good hearing, since his service was like to be needed, looking keenly on Hodgson as I said it, and he then spoke of the Nixons' attempt, but reluctantly, it seemed to me. Carleton said he had heard something of this, but it was a scratching affair, a pucker in a corner, and Bell a malcontent whining fellow. "If he has complaint at the Nixons, let him bear it to the Wardens for the next truce day, and get redress. If that likes him not, let him pay his blackmail or face the Nixons sword in hand." And this was a March officer, bound to keep the peace! But it was "the custom of the country", so I held my peace, and Hodgson would likewise but that Yarrow made some sneer at him for his fears. "You, bailiff, ye would light the beacon if a reiver let fart within twenty miles," says he, at which Hodgson in a fine rage called him dandyprat and baboon and I know not what, that knew naught of his office but drink and wenches, and was fit for no more than to cry "Give way!" at Carleton's elbow. The Land Sergeant stayed their bickering, calling it heat to no purpose.

"Give my lady a week," says he, "and if she has half her grandsire's wit she will whip Geordie Bell and such plaint-mongerers out of the parish."

Thus was Bell's business put by, as of no account, but when Hodgson came to speak of Archie Noble, that lay bound below stairs for pilfering, and suspicion of the horse that he rode, then were the officers all zeal, and Carleton wagged his head very knowing.

"Wait-about-him Noble," says he, "a petty trafficker and broken man. I have had my hand near his neck this five year, but never cause to grip him. The horse shall be looked to, there may be others, there may be more. Follow the reek and you'll find the fire. We have small matters about Gilsland that await answer; he has been about there, he may fit."

This incensed me, to hear him so eager after a petty thing that overlooked a greater mischief. "Almost I hear you say 'He will fit'," I told him.

"And if he fits a halter, Father Lewis, it will be of his deserving," said he. "We know such sturdy rogues, that

31

will neither work nor want, so shall I bear him to Carlisle."

"And there he can be borne higher yet," cries Yarrow, at which callous mockery I turned away from them, yet heard Hodgson, to his credit, intercede again with the Land Sergeant on the matter of the Bells, saying that if he would but send word into Scotland, to them that he knew of, the Nixons might be quieted. But Carleton put him off, saying his word had no weight in Scotland, which was surely a lie, for he was one that had policy and acquaintance everywhere.

I passed into the house, and presently followed the others, for it was ten o'clock and my lady still stayed for, so the bailiff, to refresh the officers, had wine brought in and a few fruits pitted and wizened with keeping. Master Carleton looked askance with a Heigh-ho and sat him down out of patience, slapping his gloves on his thigh, and spoke crossly of her late coming, for the affairs of the March could not wait, for a lady ever so noble, and "it is the curse of their light living down yonder that they think others have no greater care. Time beats a swifter measure with us than they keep in Greenwich Palace. Aye, well, my masters, she may learn, she may learn."

I was so nettled to hear his talk of care, from one that cared not for that he should have cared for, that I said boldly she had much to learn indeed, and the border was like to prove a hard school, where officers turned a blind eye on wrongs done a poor man, with not so much counsel as should stand him in small stead, and little justice save for the rich and strong, and that my heart smote me for her in her inheritance. To which he said but "Chut!" and withered me with his eye. Not so the braggart Yarrow.

32

"Gin I had her acres I'd learn me fast enough," quo' he. "Devil the broken man or family rider should set hoof on my ground."

"Fine talk in Askerton Hall," says Hodgson, that could nowise abide the deputy. "Wait thou, till thou'st ta'en a trod over Hermitage water, and seen Elwood* lances on the crest at your back, or played cat-and-mouse wi' Armstrongs in the dark on the Black Lyne –"

"Sitha, blubberguts," cries young Yarrow, "I've ridden trods enow, and sweated mair blood than thou hast fat, thou tunbelly, thou, and seen your Elwoods and Armstrongs, aye, and seen their backs, too!"

"Aye, and broke eggs wi' a stick," says Hodgson, all a-grin. "Good health, Anton, when next Ewesdale rides your way. By, we'll see grand things!"

They might have breathed themselves in such windy exchange, but now came the boy Wattie, flying: "The cotch! The cotch's coming! Father Lewis, my leddy's on the hill!" and more, in joyous frenzy, to quiet which I bade him see to the fire, it being near gone out again.

So we went out to meet her, Yarrow brushing his beard and setting his baldric so, and steel bonnet on his arm, and Hodgson in some trepidation, and myself, but Master Carleton last to rise, most leisurely patient, yet contrived to be ahead of us all, standing forth of the door. And here a great cotch, with postillions but no riders, and the kitchen folk come and the children squeaking, and all on tiptoe to see the great lady from London, with hollering of "A red bull! A red bull!" as though it had been a foray, and not my lady come into her own. Yet it seemed to me she came with no great state, but the

---

* One of the many spellings of "Elliot"

33

one cotch and two postillions, and so through the gate, and Master Carleton ready to doff and be first at the cotch door, and the bailiff coughing at my elbow, hem-hem, and scratching with his feet, and Yarrow all smiles and standing high, and myself afire to see this prodigy so long expected, and yet in the moment, that should have been so glad, felt an oppression of the spirit, I knew not why, unless it was with my contemplating of the sorry condition of all that she came into there. Howbeit, I remembered my office so long neglected, and was a priest again for the time being, though little worthy of that name. And so I fell a-praying for her, and all about me the cry of "A Dacre! A Dacre! A red bull! A red bull!"

OW, IF MASTER CARLETON hoped to puff his consequence to my lady and the world, by making show to hand her down and conduct her, he had little good of his ambition, for ere he had his bonnet off the cotch door was wide and she was by him and indoors in the blink of an eye, so that we had barely but the whisk of her cloak, and he with his hand out, into which her waiting woman a stout dame that followed after was like to give her basket, but that he made haste to withdraw in some snuff. So we must all in again, not a little abashed, and wondering at her suddenness, so that none put himself first, and 'twas myself, with Hodgson twitching at my sleeve, that led into the hall, and Master Carleton aloof behind, with, as they say here, his nose out of joint.

My lady stood before the fire, which was all but out and reeking, in which it matched her mood, as I soon saw. Yet was I mum at first, in awe of her appearance, which I had not seen such for many a year. She was of a middle height but lordly carriage, very straight and slender, and, as I thought at first, of a mould to beguile Solomon himself, so fair and pale of face like an angel in a picture, with great eyes of darkest blue, and for her hair, it was white shining gold like an infant's, which in their elders is commonly artifice, but I think hers was not. A seeming beauty, though on looking narrowly at my more time, her nose was long and her chin something pointed, yet was she handsome enough for all that, and could smile right prettily, having excellent teeth, though her wonted mien was cold and very proud, as now, with thunder between her brows. For her attire, it would have sat upon a queen, being of rare richness, to wit, a long mulberry coat with gold buttons, open at the throat, for she wore a little ruff all sewn with pearls, and above a fur beaver, daintily cocked, and on her hands a muff of like fur sable, and beneath a fine green gown shotten with gold flames that was like to set our country ladies a-gape. So was I mum, staring at such a portent female, in awe not only of her person and apparel but of that high spirit that shone from her as would have overborne the boldest, young and slight though she was. We had a taste of her salt when, I having remembered myself and bade her welcome, she gave me but a glance and cut me short with:

"Which of you is my bailiff, Hodgkin?"

At that the bailiff, dismayed to hear himself singled so bodefully, answered haltingly that his name was Hodgson, at her service, at which she demanded coldly, had he care of her tenants, to which he assenting, she let drive such an angry blast as set his teeth a-chatter, nor minded the boy Wattie then coming in with logs, who dropped them clattering at her feet, and swore, and scrambled there before her, so much was she moved.

"And will you tell me, bailiff," quo' she, "what care you have, when I find myself petitioned on the road by a poor clown with a bloodied head, got of Scotch robbers, that came to you for help, whereon you set about him

cruelly, and drove him forth with kicks? Well, sirrah –
aye or no?"

Hodgson, seeing that George Bell had been beforehand
with his grievance and kindled her to a fine rage, fell
a-tremble, and mumbled that if she would hear him –
and there his courage failed and he stood shuffling.

"What I would hear," says she, dangerously soft and
her finger tapping, "when you have done shuffling and
got your tongue, is aye or no. 'Aye, but', you say? It is
very well. We shall talk anon, Hodgson or Hodkin – nay,
never stir, shuffle yet a while." And to Wat, at her feet:
"Your logs will not get up of themselves, fellow! Gather
them, boy, to it!"

Then she threw off her back cloak and muff, and
looked about, while her maid unbuttoned her long coat,
but gave no heed to us who stood dumb, and seemed in
no great delight of what she saw, playing with her gloves
the while.

"This is all your charge, Susan," says she. "Wine and
water, and marchpane, and bid Master Lightfoot in to
me. See that this lout mends the fire without putting the
house alight, bid the grooms look to Angel and Lycidas,
for these roads are fit to kill poor beasts, and Angel limps
o' the right forefoot." And then of a sudden to Wat, that
was dropping timbers broadcast, "Oh, try again, boy,
and if you drop 'em on yon Hodgson's toes it skills not,
he shall skip of his own accord presently! 'Aye, madam,
but', forsooth! Susan, bring mine own cup, and others
for these gentlemen, for I doubt if there is a pot uncracked
this side of York. Has this place been aired in a
twelvemonth? If we are not to suffocate, put some sweet
herbs on the fire, we had as well be in a stable!"

All this in a rush of words, when, seeing my amaze,

37

she said more civilly: "Oh, sir, you wonder that I seem to take your welcome amiss, but I am in a rare fury, to see a poor man hurt, and a fat rogue blinking that gives no remedy, or even excuse, oh, it makes me mad! I thank you kindly, and these gentlemen, we shall know each other anon." And at once falls railing at Wattie, for his handlessness. "Oh, fellow, kick them before you like a football, so shall you be done sooner! Susan, bid one help him, afore he does a mischief! Now, sirs, we shall have order presently, I dare say. You, sir (this to me), by your habit should be my grandsire's papist priest. Give you good day, sir, for I will not call you father, but thank you for your courtesy. You may make these gentlemen known to me."

So I did, first Master Carleton, who with a fine bow would have come forward at leisure to address her, but she marred it for him by turning aside to Susan, which may have been by design, for it took him in his preamble, so must he start again, while my lady gave sweet apology. And then Yarrow, who smiled on her boldly and preened himself, whereat she began to eat her marchpane and bade Susan give refreshment to all of us there, and to Master Lightfoot, her man of affairs, who was come in, one of your portly sleek flat-caps with a wealth of words on both sides, not aye, not no, but mayhap, of which we had surfeit when she put to him the matter of Bell, for she seemed to set that before all, that had not yet changed her shoon, but sat forward in her great chair, cup in hand, while they strove to make all clear to her.

Now, you have heard it and need not that I weary you with it again, but I, taking no part, yet lightly marked how each spoke his side in it, save Yarrow, who was silent and left off not gaping at her like a clown at the fair when he sees the tricksters. Hodgson made poor shift to defend himself, and Master Carleton must needs instruct her, but in a lofty sort that I could see had her teeth on edge, and Master Lightfoot confirmed him on blackmail, how, albeit it was an unlawful and hateful thing, yet were poor men wont to pay, at which she cried out on them, was this how the law was kept, and Master Carleton pointed to redress before the Wardens, and that it was no great matter, and "the custom of the country", and no fault of any, save Bell himself, that looked to move my lady's pity. But ever she kept to the point, a very Portia, that here were fell thieves harassing a tenant of hers to his hurt and ruin, and how was it possible that a creature of the Dacres should pay criminal rent to such leeches, and no help at law or any way. And through all my poor bailiff knuckled his head and nay-but-madamed her, and the Land Sergeant's head higher by the moment, and Lightfoot wagging on to try the patience of a saint, and she no saint that sat there, but a lady justly moved, that I was right glad to see, yet sorry to see her at such a rough education as she could hardly believe, that here were Queen's officers of the peace, but no help from them. For Carleton budged not from saying it was not in his charge, which was for Gilsland only, not Triermain, at which the bailiff shot me a great wink of the eye, as he would say "Said I not so?"

So we had to and fro of "Nay, will my lady but hear me, she doth me wrong" and "Peace, rogue, you kicked him black and blue, go shuffle again!" and "Under correction, madam, here is great ado for a snivelling arrant fellow that hath brought the mischief on himself" and "a God's name, sir, are people of mine in thrall to Scotch thieves?" and "I did not invent blackmail, lady, nor the sorry state of the world", and "in truth, my lady, the Land Sergeant has the right of it, 'tis matter for the Wardens", and on that conclusion they fell silent, my lady a-weary and small of a sudden, and bade them bring in Bell that she would answer him.

While we waited, she said, "Susan, this chair likes me not, I had better be on the rack. Nay, let it be, the others look no better. And for dust, my barn at Blackheath is cleaner! Are there no maids in this house?" But Bell coming in, and a sorry snail he was in his rags and bloody bandage, she left off and spake him kindly, asking for his head.

"Poorly, my good lady," says he, and cringed. "But poorly. I am not young, I cannot take these knocks, please you, my lady."

She compassioned his ill-usage, and said the gentlemen had heard of it, and the Warden would see justice done on the Nixons. But at this he raised a great cry of terror that he looked not for justice, but security. "'Tis not what they've done, my lady, but what they'll do yet! They have sworn to ride on me again, and my folk and our poor beasts, aye, this night! They'll take and burn all, because I cannot pay Ill Will's tribute! Oh, my lady, I fear for my life!"

Now it was news to her that peril threatened him so close, so up starts she at Carleton, demanding was this so, and where were his watches and troopers, or was this the nether side of Russia, that a man's life and goods could be torn away? The whiles Bell pawed at her shoe, crying, "Ill Will will have us, lady, oh, sweet lady! Liddesdale never promised but performed! He'll have us! I'm Dacre's man, and served your grandsire," and the like. The Land Sergeant said again 'twas not his charge, and if he rode to every hamlet that feared a raid o' the Scots, he would never be done, and this being so, it behoved men to pay or fend for themselves.

"For themselves?" cries my lady, white as the wall. "Look at him, sir, can he fend for himself or anything? Or do you mean that I, his landlord, must take the field and fight, because your law cannot or will not?" She swore the Queen should know of it, and Carleton said, curtly enough, that Her Grace knew already. Lightfoot interposed that there was much ill, and much wrong, on the border, but it must be looked to, aye, and redress made, given time and much labour to perfection, and anon and anon, until she cried him down, and stood biting her lip to find herself at a loss what to do, and vented her rage on poor Wattie, who was at the fire, bidding him go clatter elsewhere. Then she turned on Carleton, speaking more composed, but still moved inwardly.

"Master Carleton, you cannot aid me with your office, it seems. Yet you were my grandfather's friend, and you have a name as a stout gentleman. Will you, then, not aid me as a friend, that am in sore need? I ask not the Land Sergeant, but your own self, sir."

He would need a heart of stone that resisted her (for she was fair, and brave in her distress), and then I saw Tom Carleton as near out of countenance as ever I saw, for he was a proud man, and a valiant, and but for his own policy I believe had offered his sword. To do him right, I believe he weighed in his mind what might come of fronting the Nixons, and what mischief would follow, and would have seen Bell and Triermain in Hades that put him to the choice. But a politician always, he said he might not, for it lay not in his charge, and would have spake more but she turned straight to Anton Yarrow and asked of him the same. And he stood dumb, and looked askance at Carleton, and said he might not, for he was bound by his office likewise. It choked him to say it, for he would fain have said Aye.

To my astoniment, she turned to me, and said something could be done, surely. "You are a priest," says she, "no matter what persuasion, and were these pillagers as cruel and wanton as demons, they will hardly strike where the Church protects." She said it so piteous, and her so proud, that I was near to tears to nay-say her.

"For when I was first in this country, I did such a thing, offering myself as a sacrifice, even, for the Lord's sake. And, lady, they laughed and rode by, crying 'Bless us, father', and when I cursed them, they laughed again. Oh, good lady, if you have seen the baited bear snap his chain and rush among the mastiffs, ravening, you would as well reason with him as with Ill Will Nixon and his folk, when they have a foray before them."

She made no answer, but sat her down, and fingered the crumbs upon her plate, and then called up Bell again.

"I am but lately come, and all at sea here, Master Bell," says she. "But this I tell you: you shall have security of me, your liege lord. So go up now to your place, and none shall harm you. Go." And when Bell had slobbered his thanks, and blessed her, and her grandsire, and all else that came to his mind, and gone away in wonder, rejoicing, she looked about full calm, and when Carleton and Lightfoot would have remonstrated at her, told the latter to confer with the bailiff, and give her news of the estate anon. To Carleton she inclined her head and said:

"Master Carleton and Master Yarrow, we thank you

for your courteous welcome, and look to see you again. Susan, take away my plate, and see that all is ready overstairs, for I would rest awhile. And bid our ragged Prometheus see to the fire, and build it up, for it is shrewd weather." And gave a dainty little yawn behind her hand, and fell to looking on her nails, but negligently. Carleton, being in dudgeon to find himself thus dismissed, yet kept his countenance, and giving her his leg would have gone forth silent, but the bailiff saying he had business with the Land Sergeant, by her leave, she gave him joy of it, adding that so it was business that required him not to do his duty, he should prove helpful indeed.

Carleton was like to grit his teeth at that, but she stayed him on an afterthought, saying that if it was the bailiff's affair it might be hers also, and inquired what it was.

"Why, a small thing, my lady," says Hodgson. "A loose fellow that we have below, that was taken stealing from our kitchen, that Master Carleton will carry to justice in Carel."*

"A suspect fellow, madam," says Carleton, and made to go.

Then I saw my lady's look alter, and again she stayed them, and asked if the fellow's fault was that he stole from herself.

"In effect, madam," says Carleton. "That, and sundry suspicions."

My lady smiled on him full sweetly. "Then I shall see to him here," says she. "This is my place, is it not, where

---

* Carlisle

43

I am lady lord? It behoves us, you know, to fend for ourselves in the border country."

Given tit for tat thus, he held his temper, and then was a fine fencing between them:

CARLETON: Madam, he is under suspicion, for a horse.

MY LADY: But he lies not within your charge, sir. You have many affairs, we would not burden you.

CARLETON: This is matter for the law, madam.

MY LADY: Indeed, and I have justice in my own lordship, in small affairs, do I not, Master Lightfoot?

LIGHTFOOT: Aye, my lady, but –

MY LADY: No, my lady, but! We shall look to it, Master Carleton, and at need deliver him to Carlisle. But if his offence is that he stole a pat of butter –

HODGSON: A loaf, my lady, and a cheese.

MY LADY: Jesu! Should he not go to the Warden? We must look to this, indeed!

CARLETON: Madam, this is peevish talk!

MY LADY: Bailiff, instruct the Land Sergeant that we shall weigh this matter, which lies not in his charge. And that the Lady Margaret Dacre is not scolded by common men.

CARLETON: Madam, if you look to spite me, it ill becomes you.

MY LADY: You see, Susan, these northern gentlemen know what becomes a lady. Look to thy manners, Susan – aye, seek instruction from the fellow that brings logs to the fire!

On this Carleton went, in wrath, and Yarrow at his heels, and Hodgson, at a loss, asked of her what he should do with the fellow that he had looked to see carried away.

She put him off, and, he and Lightfoot departing, she gave a great sigh and looking on me somewhat crossly, asked why so glum in my looks, and was it to see her so unwomanly towards the Land Sergeant, and taking pleasure to thwart him. Which I might not answer, I said, for presumption.

"Nay, here's a meek priest!" says she. I told her it was well for a priest to go meek, that was chaplain on sufferance to a Protestant, and she rallied me in scorn.

"The downcast eyes, the folded hands! Blessed are the poor in heart, for they shall move pity!"

I was bold to reply that she might mock me in safety, but she mocked God to her soul's peril.

"Hey, a reproof! There is some spirit in you," says she, and I marvelled to see her merry, that was so young and fair and had such unlooked for care upon her, and all within an hour of her coming in. I pondered how, being in her green years, and yet accustomed to have rule, she might on the one hand face down such masterful men as the Land Sergeant, and on t'other be a gay girl, and (what was passing strange) seem in better looks for beauty in her stern mood, than when she was pleased, or jesting. She had a good wit, and very easy, as I saw when, calling for her cloak, she bade me show her about, for she longed to see what provision there was for a garden, which indeed was a desolation behind the house, and little better in summer. She made some sallies on this, and passing to the yard, where they were burning the Christmas bays in a bonfire, called out to the maids that were by that this being Candlemass was the feast for purification of virgins, so let them that had maidenheads put on their most modest faces, for those who laughed she was sure had none, and must be handfasted presently. At which all laughed amain, and she with them, and a bold wife cried out that my lady laughing, what should they make of this? I looked to see her angered at this pertness, but not a whit, saying that if she put off the paint on her face they might see she blushed as well as any maid of them, though never so red as Mall Baty behind. They stared at this, for Mall was a woman of the place that was well known to have a great birthmark, like to St Anthony's fire, upon the cheek of her buttock, which my lady remembered to have been shown in infancy, and it seemed had borne in her memory these many years, which was a wonder indeed.

Mall was called forth, and curtsied, and all but fell down of her terror to be greeted by my lady, and then all must be called and named to her, maids and men and the elders, to their great liking. A little lass there was that, taking hold of my lady's gown, she bore her up with a "Hey, bonny!" and let her play with the gold chain at her collar, and bade Susan find sweetmeats for all the bantlings, that they might toast her return. "For," says she, "Dacre's lass that ga'd awa's coom yam, a reet lang road, an' a'." This set them in a roar, to hear the speech of their country on her lips, but presently she set down the child, and putting off something of her familiar mien, but smiling still, bade them good day, and I attending her, went within to warm herself at the fire. In admiration, I said she had given the folk much content, on which she smiled somewhat dryly and said, aye, she had put them in the hollow of her hand. This seeming a little worldly in one so young, I looked to see if she jested, but was not sure thereof.

In a while, glancing sidelong, she asked did I, being

46

a priest, look to remain in her household, "or how if I should turn you away?" I said I should go as God might direct, who had guided me in places stranger than this borderland. "And surely He is here as elsewhere, and indeed may be closer in these wild hills than in any kirk builded by men's hands."

"I have seen little sign of Him thus far," says she tartly. "We have had a deal of loving kindness this day, go to! If I should follow suit, thou'dst be through my gate, bell, book, candle, aye, and supperless!" Then smiling: "Let be, sir, you shall stay, if it sorts with your priestly conscience to serve a heretic."

As to that, I told her, I had ministered to folk of divers religions, and to some that had none, coming to believe that so God was served, the form mattered not (which indeed I do hold to most devoutly, knowing that in such a country, where life and death are nearer accomplices than elsewhere, religions must needs be made for men, and not men for religion, as our Lord taught).

"A strange priest," says she. "Well, you must not pray at me, and you shall be as delicately papist as you may with my people." Having thought a little, she said: "And if I seek your counsel, you may not presume to instruct me."

I said what service I could do she should have, gladly and in all humility, whereat she bade me sit across from her, and demanded straight: "Then tell me, of your spiritual and worldly wisdom, what I am to do for that fellow we had crouching here – the man Bell! How shall I keep my pledge made in anger before that cheeselip Land Sergeant?"

I said spiritual and worldly counsel were all one: she

47

could only pray. On which she got up, and stamped, with a good round oath, and threw her kerchief on the fire.

"Why, here's a parrot-screech after the style of those gallant gentlemen! No protection, and nothing to be done! In God's name, man, is this Arabia?"

I told her it was something worse, and the gentlemen not so cruel or craven as they seemed. The first rule of the border, I said, was that all must look to their own safety, which she could hardly do, having no tenants fit for service, for under my old lord's governance they had done none, and were grown to that condition where they would hide or run away. In time she might furnish herself a troop of proven fellows mercenary, but that could not be for tonight, when Bell must pay his blackmail or be ridden over by the thieves.

She swore yet again, and of a sudden demanded of me how much was the blackmail. I said, a few pounds, five or thereabouts, and she stood as one thunderstruck and threw up her hands.

"Jesu! And what is five pounds to me? Or fifty, if 'twill keep him whole? Good lack, he shall have the money for these caterpillars, and go scot-free for me – aye, he shall be Scot free both ways!"

I could not laugh at her jest born out of relief, but told her it might not be. "Do such, my lady, and you shall be ridden on and your riches extorted by every thief and loose man from Gretna to the Bounds of Berwick! What, the Lady Dacre pay blackmail? Some things are possible, but not that."

Her face fell like a babe's, and because she saw the force of this her anger was the greater, to be thwarted wherever she turned. She bade me void her sight in her impatience, and being without I heard a pot smash, and another, and Christ, what a nest of vipers is this, that the wolves may tear the sheep, and it must happen, welladay and be damned! – which seemed to me a great Noah's Ark in her vocabulary, yet I could not but compassion her in my heart, to be so tried and at a loss, her first day. I stayed near hand, to be of service if need be, and I confess to hear what else might pass, and the maids going in to lay out for her dinner, and Wattie to tend the fire, overheard the following:

MY LADY: What's your name, sirrah?

WAT: Wattie, Walter, an't please your grace.

MY LADY: Art grown and sturdy. Can ye fight?

WAT: Fight, my lady?

MY LADY: Aye, fight, wi' a sword! Can you fight 'gainst these ravagers, these Nixons?

WAT: Lady, I do not know. I maun do as you bid, but I have not fought afore. I've no skill in swording, but a serving-man.

MY LADY: Sweet saviour, no! Your skill is to put out the fire! Oh, get you to your logs!

WAT: Aye, my lady, surely. And shall I take the broken man his dinner?

MY LADY: Broken man, what's he?

Wattie said, the fellow she had denied Master Carleton, on which she bade him find and fetch me in, and turned her wrath on me.

"Since my great need is beyond your counsel, guide me in this nothing matter. What's to do with this pantry pirate, aside of denying him to that oily knave of a Land Sergeant? How do you deal with such?"

I said from what I heard he was a harmless fellow enough, but if he came to Carlisle he might be made to answer for more than he had ever done, being a masterless man.

"Then I am glad I was so spiteful," says she. "Sirrah Wattie, give him his dinner, and tell the bailiff to whip him and let him go. What, priest, you shake your head again?"

I said, before she judged, would she not hear him in his own behalf, that might excuse him a whipping. She looked as she would have whipped half the parish, but the maids then bringing in her dinner, said she would dine and see to him thereafter. I made no more ado, but left her, and presently Susan was gone in to oversee the service, and my lady loud lamenting that her grandsire should have set stob and stake in this godless place, 'stead of the south where were no Land Sergeants nor Nixons nor oppressed tenants nor lackaday rascal priests that shook their fat heads and spake naught to any purpose, and where had they heated this broth a Mary's name, on an ice-floe?

I pitied the broken man that was to serve for her dinner's desart (as the French say), and sought out Master Hodgson to inquire what manner of man he was, for at this time I had not seen him, but only lad Wattie's report. After particulars of his lousiness, unworth, knavery, and so forth, he told me that in person this Noble was straight and well enough if he was clean, but for now he looked as though a sheep had shitten him. Thinking that my lady might be the worse disposed towards a draggled dirty fellow, I besought the bailiff, out of charity, to give him water to wash at least, and other to mend his appearance, for, said I, a razor to his face may save him a lash to his back, nor will she thank you to present her a rascal all bemired and filthy. This last determined him, and he went forthwith to see it done, but hearing more clatter from the hall, and loud miscalling of the cook for a rank poisoner, and the Nixons and Bell and the Land Sergeant all in a breath, I doubted my good intentions would be vain in the end.

HE DINNER BEING by my lady called not for Noble to be haled up, and Susan told me she purposed to go a-riding, to see the home farm, and was gone up to change her habit. One had been sent to Naworth to fetch her palfrey left behind with the second and third cotches, these having all her gear and goods, so now I saw why she had come in with such little state, for these cotches were heavy and slow. I saw the palfrey brought in, and an airy white beast it was, bred and proud as its owner, and the people a-gape at its costly tackle of silver and stamped leather, and the page that held it a pretty shaveling that looked mighty disdain of these common folk. They gaped the more when my lady came down breeched and booted like a boy in doublet and hose of crimson, with a little feather cap and hair bound in a net. Such fashion was not seen in the north, nor yet I believe at the Court, but I have heard that in the west country it is seen where ladies do wear it for convenience and ease, or as I think more likely to show off their fine shape, if they have one. The women fell a-whispering and gleeking among themselves, but she marked it not and talked to the page that fed tidbits to the palfrey.

She would have been away but Hodgson coming said he had brought up the broken man, and what was her will of him. She was ill pleased, and said there was no peace to be had, but seeing the bailiff shuffle and stutter mayhap soothed her sulk, for she tossed her switch to the page bidding him stay for her, heaved a sharp sigh, and strode within like an angry trooper, pulling off cap and gloves and sat her down straight, bidding Hodgson "bring in the crust-picker".

So now I had my first sight of this Archie Noble the Waitabout that was to turn my life's course, who was then naught to me yet because I had been at some pains to see him decently arranged I looked at him the more jealously. He was of a good gangling stature, more than two yards tall but a little stooping, perhaps inclining to forty years, for his hair which was fair was gone back from his brow save the widow's peak that some say is a sure sign against drowning (from which they conclude he is gallows-bound, that being their superstition). His face was long and large as to chin and jaw, not uncomely and looked keenly, for his eye was bright blue and very open, of that seeming candour which to my mind oft conceals more than if his lids were closed. A strange thing that I marked in him was that he was of those who seem to take more space in a room than their body has need of, as they had an invisible presence beyond their limits, which has not to do with apparel or station or any manner put on, but is of their being. For that which covered him I may not call it clothing, so sorry a sight he was, being in ragged breeks and cracked boots, and no shirt but a sleeveless jack of leather such as the riders wore, sewn with plates of horn for defence of which it lacked not a few.

Hodgson led him by his hands bound behind, and set him before my lady, and methought he gave back, looking to see a woman and beholding what seemed at first shot to be a stripling boy, yet when he made out what she was kept his countenance and gave her the look direct. She of her part looked curiously on him, to see one so outlandish and beggarly that cast not down his eyes before her, she not then knowing these borderers who give eye for eye with any whatsoever their quality. And of this I will take oath, that in the moment there was betwixt them a sort of knowing of each the other, such as happens rarely between two at first glance, though they be as far apart as the poles in nature and upbringing and experience or any other thing. I call it not an understanding nor a sympathy nor attraction nor any of the sensibilities with which we may regard one another (though I saw those at work in them before all was done), but fall again on the poor word "knowing", which I can explain no better.

Now, whether for that, or that he was a likely fellow enough for all his rags that stood before her civilly, not abashed but with a half-bold, half-droll aspect that seemed to mock not others but himself, my lady looked on him more kindly, and speaking lightly as she toyed with her cap's feather, and called him "larder poacher", asked his name.

He seeing her so young and studying to please her, answered with that ready wit he had, making play upon his name. "Noble, my lady. Or Noble, my noble lady. Noble lady, my name is Noble. A simple Noble, yet Noble, noble lady."

This pleasantry unlooked for in such a fellow that should have been in terror for his plight, put her in a little maze, saying was the man mad, at which Hodgson said, not mad, but impudent, and fell to cuffing him and

54

bade kneel to the lady. She told him to strike when she bade him, not before, and wherefore was the fellow bound.

"Why, think on, my lady," says Hodgson. "'Tis a dangerous arrant rascal."

"That steals bread and cheese," says she, "and looks none so dangerous to me." Then considering the prisoner, to see I think if he had more quips at command, asked him was he dangerous or no.

"Godamercy, lady," says he, "I think I danger only myself, since 'twas my folly that brought me to this pass. And I had better stay bound, for if of your gracious gentleness ye were to loose me, my gratitude might lead me to speak more than I should, for I have a too-ready tongue, and would not give offence."

"That you have given already," says she, "and master bailiff has a sharp cure for it. What, thou hast plundered my kitchen, knave, and yet you give pert answers and smile and look me in the eye!"

"Why, my lady, you are my judge, so where else should I look?" says he. "And if I looked elsewhere, ye'd take it as a poor compliment. And if I smile, 'tis in the hope of winning your kind opinion."

Now this was said with such a droll humility that for all his readiness my lady was like to smile herself, knowing that he practised on her, yet liking him none the worse for it. Yet being female she must play with him a little, so looked on him less kindly, sitting back in her chair and feigning displeasure.

"Shalt not win it by insolence," says she. "Look you, Master Kitchen Thief, if you value your back's skin, study to please me, for I have care enough to be most infernally vexed, what with big-bellied bailiffs and milky-mealy priests and give-me-leave-lady officers and hand-less louts that cannot mend a fire and scabby reivers that grin and gird at me. In short, I am in no good humour, but inclined to sulk and send any nimble-tongued humble-insolent rascal to the whipping-post to vent mine anger. So look how you try to melt me; shalt not melt Master Hodgson's whip hand!"

The bailiff saw not that this seeming peevishness was less than earnest, and laying hold on Waitabout begged my lady to let him have at him, and was told to keep his place and shuffle a while longer. "Well, fellow, tell me why I should not let him have his way with you, that stole from my kitchen."

"By your leave, lady," says Waitabout, "I stole not, for your varlets capped me or ever I might e'en say grace – nay, lady, this is not impudence, but mere truth to illustrate *quam prope ad crimen sine crimine.** Yet if I plead that, you will think I mock at you, so hadst best whip me and ha' done."

"In good time," says she, nodding, but not a little astonished. "And where got you Latin?"

"From Father Gilpin of Tynedale, him they called Gallows Priest for that he shrived most at the gibbet-foot. His acolyte I was, and like to have been priest myself, but . . ."

"But what, knave?" says my lady, eager to hear.

"Why, in truth," says the bold villain, looking droll, "I must get him communion wine, out o' Scotch abbeys, and was ta'en in the lifting of it. Which was no sin, surely, being of the enemy and no more than King Harry did in England that took not only the wine but the abbeys

* How close a man may come to guilt without being guilty.

56

it lay in. Aye," says he, wagging his head, "I lifted me more than your bailiff could sup in a twelvemonth." At which insolence she was surprised into laughter outright, seeing Hodgson enraged, and the jester who knew well how to cap his own sally, said if she doubted his former priestliness she might see its tokens in his present condition, poverty and humility.

"And what of chastity?" asks my lady, more sidelong than I liked. "Art chaste, rogue?"

"The length o' the border, lady, from Annan to Alnwick!" says he, at which she laughed again, and he asked had he pleased her.

"Enough for the bread and cheese," says she, and bade Hodgson let him go, with sixpence for his sauciness. Which, though I found him overbold and lacking reverence, yet I was pleased to see that lenity in her which befits those that have rule, but is not found always. Not so Hodgson, who being nettled by Waitabout's wit said there remained the suspicion of the horse he rode, that might be stole. My lady drawing on her gloves to be away said it was all one to her if he had stolen York Minster, and would have put the matter by, but Hodgson clamouring it must be inquired on for the public weal, she bade Waitabout answer her briefly how it was got.

"Why, lady," says he, "what's my horse to do wi' anything?"

She said naught for her part, but the Land Sergeant would be satisfied, so he should answer. To this Waitabout swore the horse was his own, but having no proof nor paper thereto he had liefer not answer at Carlisle for it, where they were wont to hang poor men upon suspicion only.

This sorting with what she had heard before she railed

out again upon a law that would do as much yet could not secure tenants against forayers, "so shall you answer to me, and not to that long-nose Carleton. Make me oath on't and shalt see that in my manor innocence may walk unafraid."

Now was he out of countenance, yet sought to mask it with a jest that on the border innocence did better to creep by unnoticed, and if he spoke truly of the horse she would think worse than if he lied. Seeing him palter, her brows came together, and "I'll think worst of all, sirrah, if ye put me off further."

This put him in a strait, but having no help for it he made reluctant oath that he had gotten the horse on the Scotch side but two nights since, of one Dod Pringle, a great thief of Teviotdale that he had chanced on in the waste. Hodgson swore disbelief, how had Pringle that was a stark rider and notable villain parted with such a fine hobbler to a vagrom broken man?

At this Waitabout shuffled and looked askance and drew breath, and would have said no more, but being pressed said that the Pringle had been one of a Scotch raid pursued out of England by Warden men, and being separated from his fellows and coming unaware on Waitabout that was bedded in the bracken, "so Black Dod, out of wits with the pursuit, and knowing himself for a murderer and worse, came raging on me wi's lance, and having no help for it I must defend myself."

Again he gave over his tale, while we looked on him amazed, and Hodgson asked had he killed the Pringle, which Waitabout confessed he had, and taken the horse for fear of pursuit, and lain him up in the waste until hunger brought him forth to our door.

Seeing my lady turn paper colour and thunderstruck,

and myself at a loss before his bloody relation, Waitabout sought to excuse the deed in the telling, with such terms as "carefully" and "by chance" and "out of no malice", which was a misjudgment, being so like to that irony he used in jesting, and far from apology made it sound worse, as though he lightly regarded the taking of life. Which I am sure he did, being bred in a hard school. But if my lady and I stood speechless awhile for the horror of it, and so easily told, not so Hodgson who let fly a great oath.

"Yon Scotch gallows-bait! Now here's the best news this twelvemonth! Slain Black Dod! Why, man, hast done a service! For this Pringle," he told my lady, "was a right filthy fellow and man-killer, a curse in God's sight, and saving my lady's presence, overdue damnation from's cradle!" And heartily asked Waitabout what ailed him, Black Dod being so foully regarded of both sides that the Land Sergeant would give him good deliverance.

Waitabout doubted this, the Pringle being approved of Kerr of Cessford, and Master Carleton unwilling for policy to offend such a puissant Scotch lord, but as he spoke I marked rather how my lady and Master Hodgson had gone widdershins in their opinions, the bailiff now liking Waitabout whom he had ill-eyed before, while my lady, that had smiled on him kindly but a moment since, now looked as one that knows not what she hears, passing to loathing and horror, which Waitabout seeing protested his honesty to her. She gazed on him as though he were a very toad.

"This passes for honesty?" cries she. "I ask a fellow how he came by a horse, and he says 'Fie, madam, 'tis a nothing matter, I had it by cutting a throat o' Monday night.' And this for an honest answer! Am I run mad or

59

is this Bedlam? Oh, but I forget – this is Cumberland, where a man may stand open-eyed and talk of murder as though 'tis no more than rifling a jam-pot! And my priest crosseth himself welladay, and my bailiff his great guts quiver with admiration! Now, save me, for I know nothing!"

At this Hodgson begged her bethink this was at worst a manslaughter, and I must needs speak, indeed to assure her how I abhorred the act, and deplored it, but that, alas, as the border judged these things, it was common enough, and in their phrase, the custom of the country. This put her in such a taking that I never saw such white heat from a fair vessel.

"Jesu! And I forebore to whip him for bread and cheese! And would have dealt kindly with a poor harmless knave that stood this half hour smiling and beguiling and jesting of little faults, and now, on's own confession, I find he's bloody as Cain! And a priest to excuse it, and that shuffling thing to applaud it – oh, aye, since 'twas a Scotch throat cut, what's to matter, murder or manslaughter, 'tis all one! Well, your distinctions are too nice for me. Let him to Carlisle, where as the border judges they may knight him for his butchery, or if not, hang him up for it, or for the horse, or for lacking a patch to his breeches arse – for that, like enough, will be the custom of the country!"

And she flung her cap on the fire that had consumed her kerchief, and when I sought to calm her telling her it was ill to understand by one of her sex gently nurtured that came unknowing into a hard country, she rounded on me with a great oath that she could understand the Barbary rovers better. She bade Hodgson take his prisoner out and hold him for the Land Sergeant, "who if his justice bears as hard on him as it doth on other slayers and flayers, these Nixons that threaten me and mine, he has little enough to fear. God's light, it seems that in these parts none dare harm a thief save another thief!" And forthwith strode to the door, calling "Hola, Peterkin!", but as the page came tripping to see what was her will, she bore up stock-still, and her rage seemed to die like a candle snuffed. She stood with her hands clasped, as one in a muse, and I wondered at this change and waited to see if the storm should rise again, but it did not.

Thus stood she while I might tell two paternosters, when collecting herself and seeing the page that knelt by her, waiting her will, she fell to toying with his hair that was spry and curly, and smiled to herself in such wise that I felt a sudden fear chill to my marrow, such an ill smile and out of all keeping with her moods past that I had seen come and go camelion-like. But when she spoke it was gently to the page, taking the switch from his hand and bidding him see her palfrey well stalled for she would not ride today. She bade him also send Master Lightfoot in to her, but even as he sped on his errand called him back, and said he should let the lawyer alone "for it were best we made shift without his counsel, since he is one that understandeth not the custom of the country."

Now at these words my fear increased, so bodeful they sounded in her utterance. Hodgson trembled to hear her, and Waitabout his breath rustled like an asthma as though he read his doom in them, the which I doubted not she had the stomach to, for now she looked on him cruelly out of that fair cold face, tapping the switch on her hand and saying nor would she trouble the Land Sergeant "whose cares are so heavy that he must snore abed even when poor folk are rid on to their ruin. Sure, we must relieve him of this paltry fellow, and take him in our charge."

And pacing slowly to the table of a sudden struck it a great stroke with her switch which she let lie there, while we stood dumb. Then putting her arm a-kenbo asked Hodgson what trees stood about the house.

Fearing her intent, he stammered ere he could answer that there were many fair trees, and she asking him in particular, said there were many ash and chestayne, with oak and elm beyond the barnekin.

"Oak will serve," says she, with that ill smile again. "'Tis a sturdy tree and most English. You are English, are you not, sir murderer? But if the chestayne likes you better, why, 'tis all one. What say you?"

My flesh crawled to hear her so mildly spoke yet fell smiling, and crawled yet again to hear Waitabout try to put on a brag though his voice was hoarse, answering that chestaynes had ever been dear to him having in childhood used their nuts for toys. I would have sued with her, but she bade me right harshly hold my peace.

"I am lord in my own manor with justice therein," said she. "And if you open your mouth to me I shall have you thrashed out of bounds, by God I will!"

Then told the bailiff to put him below, and furnish an hurdle and rope, and for me I might keep my words for Master Waitabout if he had need of them, which, she said, she doubted not, "for if his sinful tally be no more than one slaughter and horse reft, oh, aye, and bread and cheese intended, I'll be the more astonished." And so left us.

HEN SHE WAS GONE out the bailiff and I were like men of stone, to have heard her that had seemed so civil and toward a lady, if impetuous, condemn in such malice and almost in jest, but Waitabout although something pallid as well he might be, wagged his head and said she was her grandsire's get, and no gainsaying. We looked on him in terror, but when I offered him to do such service as I might for his soul, shrugged it away saying it availed him not for the time, but if, like Gilpin of Tynedale, I would minister at the gibbet foot, it might do him some good.

I remonstrated with Hodgson that was indeed shaken now though he had shown little regard for his prisoner before, but was taken aback by this sudden cruel resolve in my lady. Better, I said, that he should acquaint the Land Sergeant quickly, so might Waitabout stand on trial for what he had confessed, but this he would by no means listen to for his office's sake. "I have seen that this past hour that I have not seen the like since my old lord was in his fiery youth! I durst not, Father Lewis, for I know yon look, and that hellish humour. And, man, it is her right, were Carleton and Warden and all against her, saving the Queen's grace." Which he fell to muttering he doubted they would, but would approve her proceeding on Waitabout, whom he then led down, leaving me in much agony of spirit, no more for him that was to suffer than for her that showed such little ruth, unseemly in one so young and of her sex.

I got me to prayer, but I fear rustily – no, I am and was no priest at all. Still it seemed to me that a poor intercession were better than none, so I russled at it in my chamber, and presently was much amazed to hear one singing on a gay note right careless, thus:

> So Charlie shall have a new bonnet,
> And Charlie shall go to the fair,
> And Charlie shall have a new ribbon
> To tie up his bonny brown hair.

I went down, and here is my lady all smiles, and in a pretty day gown of blue, bearing a new pomaunder which she called out I must prove for her, putting it to my nose saying that Susan had come on a sacket of lavender for her. If my flesh had been plucked before, it was like now to creep from my frame to see her so blithe, knowing what she purposed, and I fell to wondering was she one of those that, seeming fair and pleasant, yet have that cruel lust that joyeth in the torment of others, as ye may see not in men alone, but even more in ladies that I have observed laugh loud and high when the mastiff tears the bear's flesh, or peep 'twixt their fingers eagerly when Derrick is at his employ with the bowelling knife.

It put me in fresh fear of her, yet would I have spoken, but she bade me gently enough hold my peace, and sit, for I should have stirring enough anon. This I did, to one side, while she told me that she would soon have brought up from London furnishings and costly stuffs and fitments that would make this mouldy cave, as she called it, a house fit for the Queen's grace herself if she should ever fare north, in which case, says she with a roguish look, "you must put off your habit and beads and look like a Christian." So she sat in her great chair humming hey-nonny and talking lightly, and breathing in her pomaunder until Hodgson came, leading the Waitabout bound, who made a bow to my lady and kept his countenance, but not with much ease.

She putting by her pomaunder, looked fixedly upon him a while, and asked had Hodgson set the hurdle and rope by the chestayne. "For here is one that hath confessed to life taken, and a horse carried away, and breaking in, that are all felonies commonly punished by death. And since he falleth in my charge my duty is plain to see." At this I would have broken in, but she stilled me with a hand raised, and still considering Waitabout, asked of Hodgson, was the Scotch knave that had died untimely a great thief indeed. At this the bailiff, thinking she sought some excuse in Waitabout's favour, cried out eagerly:

"Lady, as stark a rogue as ever fired thatch! A' slew and robbed along the line, and slaughtered severals and carried off mair insight and did mair mischief –"

"I meant not that," says she. "So great his crimes, yet he was as much a life to answer for as any. I meant rather, was he a stout man of his hands?"

Hodgson wondering swore he was all of that, and for sword or lance Dod Pringle had been the master of all but a scant few, aye, saving perhaps, says he, babbling in his fashion, Willie Kang the Irvine, or Jack Charlton, or now he thought on't, Geordie Burn or young Rob

Carey that was Middle March Warden for England, until she cut him short.

"Then to kill and rob him was no small thing," says she, and looked narrowly on Waitabout what time she sighed in her pomaunder again. "Tell me, fellow, that stand doomed and can make not bad worse: how many more have ye slain in your time – oh, gently defending yourself?" And in that instant I wondered whither she went, that aimed not where she looked, and Waitabout's shrewd wit mayhap wondered too, for he answered with somewhat of his droll face.

"Nay, an't please my lady, I have opened my mouth over-wide this day, and would keep modest silence."

At which, after a moment, she gave a little sigh again. "Then fare ye well, Master Waitabout." And to Hodgson: "Hang him up." And rising would have gone briskly out, but Waitabout, seeing his life walk away with her dainty steps, cried out what would she have of him that baited him with questions. She looked not back until at the very door, when he calling again what would she have of him, she turned about.

"Come, that's better," says she. "What would I have? In a word, yourself. Your service, which I would not choose, but I have no otherwhere to turn." She came to him, and looked upon his face, and spake flat and plain. "Serve me, and you shall have life. Deny me, and you hang."

"Lady, a God's name," says he, and his voice shook, rather with wonder than fear. "How serve you?"

"At this place Triermain," says she. "Against the thieves that will ride on my tenants this night."

Then I saw all that had half-guessed at it before, and my soul rejoiced for her who had been but playing to bring him into that terror she would have him in, for her purpose, and then I trembled for what might come of it, and cried out with the bailiff that she bethink what she said, at which she turned on us right fierce.

"I think what I do! Needs must I, that have no other help but mine own wit! It lies all in my charge, as I have been well instructed this day." And again came that ill smile. "On this border men must shift for themselves. It is the custom of the country."

Hodgson protested that this was a broken man, a wanderer of no account.

"That can fight thieves!" cries she. "So he can make a stand against these Nixons for me, do I care if he is Bayard or the village idiot?"

Waitabout bewildered asked what of the Nixons, and Hodgson telling him briefly, he looked on my lady in amaze, and then said here was a fair choice, to hang on her gibbet or die such a death as the Nixons would give him if he withstood them. My lady in anger said that he might to the chestayne now and the devil thereafter, for if he liked not the choice she would make a balladine* of him then and there. He shook his head as one that understands not, and said he was but one, and would she have him face many?

"Aye," says she. "That, or face your Maker."

He nodded two or three times slowly, regarding her as though to judge her resolve, and then asked, had she thought of what avail would one poor March rider be against those lusty reivers, monstrous men such as she knew not of, "or have ye thought that I might take your service and turn tail afore I was a mile from your house?

* comic dancer

67

Nay, but ye have wit enough to judge me true that asks the question." Of Hodgson he asked how many Nixons would ride. The bailiff answered five or six, never more than ten, and the Waitabout sighed and grated his teeth.

"So," says he, "there will be Ill Will, and with him Clemmie the Clash and Half-drowned Geordie, and Hungry Jock Nixon also. But no Armstrongs or Crosers?"

"Not this road," says the bailiff. "It is Ill Will's blackmail."

Waitabout considered, as one that reckons in his mind, and we all quiet and myself mightily troubled, but my lady spake not nor took her eyes from him. He put his head of one side and asked her, if he said her nay would she hang him up indeed? Still she answered not but ever looked on him, and again I felt that knowing between them. At length he smiled and took a great breath and said:

"God willing, lady, I'll keep your village for you."

Hearing this, I besought her take counsel of the Land Sergeant at Gilsland or the Captain of Bewcastle, urging that a raid resisted might prove worse than if she let the reivers have their will of the place, and Hodgson cried this up too, and all the while she looked on Waitabout and seemed to hear us not. Then of a sudden she said was this our counsel, to leave her folk defenceless 'gainst the wolves, and was that the custom of the country? We were silent, and she asked Waitabout could he make the village good? He asked her what men she had, and she said, none that would not fly when the fray rose, they being but her page and postillions and the menials of the house.

"Then I must put some metal in your tenants, lady,"

says he, "and there my heart doubts me, for what I know of them they are sheep. But, there. You are resolved on this thing?"

She said she was. Then, said he, for his life he would serve her until next day sunrise, and she must stand assurance for him to the Wardens for any harm done, and compensate him for the loss of his horse, should it so befall, and answer any complaint or bill brought by any against him, and use her good offices at law if need be. She opened her eyes at this catalogue and bade him take breath.

"Do you make terms with me that can put you to the gallows?"

"What better time to make terms, lady?" quo' he. "It is the custom of the country."

She looked to us, and Hodgson said it was so, and she consented, so that he kept his bargain, of which he must make oath.

He called on Hodgson to loose his hands that were bound this while, which being done he spat in his right palm and held it forth to my lady, saying: "Archie Noble, called Wait-about-him, till morrow sunrise."

Again she looked to us, and I told her, though my heart was like lead for this rash proceeding, that it was their way, and if she took his hand in a like clasp there should need no other oath. So she put out her small hand that I marvelled to see tremble, but he took it not, and she understanding made a little spit in her palm, and was a moment confused (and I think displeased) before she put it forth again. Which being done he held it yet a moment and, stooping quickly, kissed it, which to me was the greatest wonder of all. She asked what did he need for Triermain, and he said so she made him free of

69

the armoury and stables she need no further care, and begged leave to withdraw "for there is much to do if I am to be in Triermain by day-go-down. Save you, lady."

She turned and went straightway to the window, and he begged me attend him in the armoury presently. Supposing he meant to make confession I assented, and he being gone, was minded to speak to my lady, though hardly knew in the tumult of my thoughts what to say, or that it would do good. And as I waited, came the lout Wattie, that had been by the door all unnoticed, who after some loitering crept to her softly at the window, and there down on his knees by her. Seeing her occupied he gave little coughs and grunts and made bold to touch her hem, at which she looked frowning and asked him what he did there.

"To serve you, lady," says he, and wiped his great nose and stammered but took never his eyes from hers. "I cannot fight in arms nor sword at all, Lady Madge, but I'll do as the broken man bids me, Lady Madge, Lady Madge."

"Why call you me that?" she asked, and he said he had ever done, at which she looked perplexed and shook her head, and I saw her thoughts were elsewhere. The clown put up his hand, but timidly, and she not thinking took it, at which he fell to slobbering her fingers with kisses, and called her again Lady Madge, Lady Madge, which I thought to disgust her, for he was foul. And indeed she took her hand away, but gently, and bade him mend the fire.

I SOUGHT HODGSON presently that was in the buttery washing his wits, so shaken was he at what had passed and was to come, and put it to him what might be done to turn my lady from her purpose. But I had as well talked to the wind that dries my shirt, for he shook like one in an ague, full of frightened oaths, and cried out that she would have her way surely, so let it be and come what might, it was not for us to cross her or meddle anyways. When I spoke of the Land Sergeant he swore the matter was no one's charge but my lady's, and for fear of her he durst not send word to Carleton nor yet the Warden himself, "for she is set, by God, and let what will fall at Triermain, aye, if she set the March in a blaze, 'tis her own affair and we but servants well quit on't. God help us, God help us," and so to his pot again to drown his fears in October.

So I betook me to Waitabout in the armoury in the old tower, and found him sat against the wall putting an edge to a broadsword and sang to himself in the fashion they have, being great spinners of songs and rhymes upon anything. It was an old song, he said, and apt to the occasion.

I hear it told on the borderside
That some maun walk and some maun ride
And some will fly and some will stay
But a Dacre never runs away.

The which, he said smiling, we had the proof of. I
wondered to find him so blithe who went soon on such a
venture, but he answered me that one who has sat in
the Lickingstone Cell minds not the Castle guardroom,
meaning, from a proverb they have in Carlisle, that he
having been near put to the gallows looked on the peril
of the Nixons as a lesser evil. The thought of which set
me shaking in despair for him that must ride that road,
and minding why I came there to comfort him, I asked
would he now make his confession, in especial for that
Pringle he had slain with all his sins on his soul, so he
had died unprepared. He answered smiling that Black
Dod had died "unexpected" but not "unprepared", a
different thing, "for see thou, father, there be two sorts
of men prepared for death always, your saints that know
themselves clean of all wrong, and your men of blood
that have ridden long with Death grinning at their elbow,
so are they ever ready for him, what of gallows or sword
or drowning-pit or what you will."

I told him it was no time to chop words lightly, and
it lay heavy on him that Pringle had died unshriven for
his immortal soul sake, to which he said scandalously
that Black Dod had no more soul than Granny Storey's
pig, so let it be, he was ready for hell-fire that same
Pringle, if he believed in it, which Waitabout said he
doubted that he did.

Such blasphemy had moved me to anger once, yet I
had heard the like and often in the border country, for

the truth is that while the half of them are of the Old Faith or the New the other half are the veriest pagans, as I told you before of their wicked jest that said they were no Christians but Armstrongs and Elwoods. I had not looked to find him such, that had by his own account been schooled by Gilpin of Tynedale, that was a good priest if something savage by report. So I spoke him gently, saying that the Pringle's belief was more than he knew for, and a soul he had for all that, but it had passed unshriven. He said that might be, yet Black Dod had no thought to it, "for at the last 'twas not for a priest he cried, but only 'Thou? Thou, Archie Noble, bastard thou! Not fit, man, not fit!' For seest thou, father, 'twas unexpected to him, as I told thee, that such as I should be his bane, and galled him sore. But of his soul he thought not at all."

I rebuked him that this was rambling talk and unseemly, yet in the heart of me I marvelled, and do yet, to hear a stark man bred of that border tell me that in the deed of slaying he had looked in the other's eyes and thought to see what lay within. I told him it was no matter for that, for whatever of the Pringle, he now had his own soul to make, and he must confess himself to me.

He said he would not, nor had ever done, and if soul he had it was his own and he would make it his own way, "as I told Father Gilpin and was cast out wi' a right grand cursing, yet he blessed me, too, for that was his way."

Keeping to my road I remonstrated to him, and spake of God and the damnation that awaited those who were not within His grace, as he was not that would go presently into death's shadow, and he laughed and asked did

73

I know the tale of the old reiver that forayed the Hell road? I would have shut my ears to this, but he asked again did I know the tale, and at the last I must even listen.

There was an old reiver, he said, away back in the time before the saints came to the borderland and the folk knew not God but their own heathen spirits. He had voyaged o' horseback three score years and more, doing great spoil and murder, but now was greatly aged beyond his tribe, his old gangers being long dead and he solitary. When the saints came bringing in the Gospel, and baptised many, they sought out the old reiver and told him of the Faith and of repentance and absolution and salvation assured, if he would be baptised. The which pleased him until, the moment of baptism being come, he asked what of his old riding comrades long dead, how should they, not being baptised, have salvation. The saints told him that such were damned to eternal torment in Hell for their horrid lives, but he repenting and being baptised might be saved. "Then I'll none o' your baptism," says the old reiver. "Nay, man, Hell road or any other, I ride wi' my gang."

And having done, asked me, would my God turn His face away from the old reiver, "for if ye say 'Aye, He would', as I know ye must, then I tell ye straight, father, He is no God for me."

At this I gave way to anger, and told him his parable was of the Devil and a fitting godless legend for a godless folk, at which he laughed and said he had it from Father Gilpin himself, "who was as good a priest as you, surely. And taught me God is love, yet asked did any man have greater love than the old reiver?"

Seeing myself mocked and knowing not how to answer,

I said bitterly he had gotten himself little good from this same Gilpin and asked what other blasphemy he had learned him, for I was in a rage at his gibes and deceits. He put off his droll face, and said he had done him great good, teaching him his letters, and much besides from three books that he kept ever by him, one being a Latin Bible, and another the Babees Booke "from which he taught me to keep sharp my knife to cut honestly my own meat, and drink not with a full mouth, which had I minded when gluttoning in my lady's kitchen this night past, I had not been taken likely." Gilpin's third book, he said, was the Travels of John Mandeville, full of wonderful tales, and asked me "that have been about the world, are they true or no, the basilisks and the Head Right Hideous, and the folk that go upon the one foot, hey, father?"

Knowing again that he mocked, yet I answered him, they were not true for aught that I had seen, but that all things were possible.

"Aye," says Waitabout, "God and the Anthropophagi both," and then begged my pardon if he had given offence by his lightness, "for it were best we left talk of God, which can only be uncomfortable between us." But if I wished to say Mass for the Pringle's soul, he would pay the shot, if he came through the night's work at Triermain.

I marvelled at the man who was such as I never saw nor heard before, that spake blasphemy with an easy smile, yet when I looked into his eyes could see no fault there, and wondered was he the Devil in a fair shape, yet knew him in my heart to be a man as other men. I knew not what to make of him that had so disturbed my poor mind, and gave me mighty distress of spirit for giving me to think what should not be thought upon, yet this only I knew, that speak and seem and be what he would, I might put trust in him as in no other that I ever knew, for good or ill.

While we spoke, he was about the armoury and ratching through the gear there, and plain to see he was at work that he knew and liked well, smiling and whistling as he assayed what of spears and swords and lances, weighing them in his hand and proving points and edges right soldierly, trying sundry knives and poniards, looking thoroughly to dags and calivers with their shot and powder, and said there was gear enough to face a Scotch army, could fit men be found for them. "And whether the Bells be such, God alone knoweth."

Then turned on me, leaning on a lance, and regarded me a long while, and I silent in my trouble for what he had said before and my grief of knowing that I could do him no good by my office. Then spoke, telling me that he could no ways to Triermain alone, for that the folk would not heed him that was less than themselves, "unless some better person come to give assurance that I am in my lady's service and stand for her. The bailiff I'll none of, for he is one that would make bad worse in dealing with the Bells, and I doubt besides if oxen could draw him from Askerton this night. So," and looked on me with his crooked smile, "I must lean on the Church which is strong and endureth. Will ye to Triermain, Father Lewis, and speak my lady's desire? They will heed you. And being come, you had best bide, for when all's done you will still find much to do."

Now as God sees me I would have said him nay but could not, for detest as I might the fell compact made 'twixt my lady and him, yet what he said was true, and

76

I only could lay it open to the Bells what he came for, and was her man to direct them. Unless my lady herself had gone to lay command on them, but at this he shook his head.

"She must bide here, and that's ower close to the fray for my liking. I'd bid her to Carel, but she's the owd dog's bitch and would not go. Or would she heed you, father?"

I said she would not, and need not, for the Nixons would dare no attempt on her person, being of such consequence.

"Get away!" cries he, in that scorning way they have. "Man, Ill Will Nixon would lift Our Lady o' Carel herself if a' thought there was ransom or advantage in't! And she'd not be the first, neither, as Percy's lady could tell thee." By which he meant the Countess of Northumberland that was held by the Liddesdales and sore mistreated in the great rising. "Well, aye, a' the March kens by now that Dacre's lass is hame, and if Triermain was to fall the night, why, 'tis none so far on to Askerton, as the Nixons ride."

This put me in great alarm for her sake, but again he shook his head and bade me be quiet.

"Triermain'll not fall," says he. "Not this road. So, father, will ye go with me?" And though I would fain have had no part in it, as a thing unbefitting, and to tell truth for my terror of the Nixons, yet I consented, and asked what order he would take at Triermain, for it seemed to me (who had seen something of like work in Mexico) that if he could put some stomach into the Triermains, to make a show enough, the Nixons might think better of their attempt, and no blood be spilled. He looked hard on me a moment.

77

"Why, that's to be seen, father. But I tell you I go as 'twere to Flodden Edge, aye, ready for a fray. *Pacem volens, parans bella*, seest thou," and now took much care in choosing two bow staves, bending them behind his thigh and weighing the draw when he had strung them, most yeomanly, and shafts also of which he waxed the heads. To see this arming of so much tackle put me in dismay, yet out of curiosity I asked what need of bows when he had pieces enough to shoot with. He answered that he would trust to no pieces that might misfire on a damp night, "and besides a man that minds not a popgun at his breast will fall to thinking of bed and safety when ye cover him wi' a cold chisel head on a yard of ash. Aye, father, 'tis wonderful how they fear the long bow yet!"

When he had gathered the gear together, with a few steel caps and jacks, he called the lad Wattie and bade him take all down to the barnekin gate, and then go quietly to the stable for an ass to carry it, and bring also his own horse and another to the gate. The clown was all eager, and would have sought leave of the bailiff, but Waitabout forbade.

"Let him be, and my lady also. If none should see you, 'tis no matter, and if any should ask, tell 'em you do her bidding. Away, now, as secret as you can, for the light will go soon, and I would have of it what I may."

I asked should we not see my lady afore we went, and he swore he would as soon take leave of the parish council "that change their minds but once each quarter hour, so my lady may prove a weathercock like all her sex, and like as not will repent her design and put my neck in a halter again. We have our gear and our charge and a clear way to Triermain; 'tis enough."

Such hasty proceeding put me in a swither that two

hours since had had no thought but supper and bed, and now found myself rushed away by this active fellow. But I protesting, he told me shortly that I might stay or go, but it must be now, and busied himself putting a shirt under his jack, with a steel cap or salade, and girding on a sword and poniard. I put off my habit and shoes and took boots and a cloak, and on his advice a steel cap also, which I no wise wished, but he said none but a fool would venture on such an errand with less. "If it sorts not with your calling," says he, "mind that the Nixons sort not with it either. And seeing you accoutred, the Triermains are the more like to accoutre themselves." He would have had me take a weapon also against the need of defence, but this I would not do, telling him that on no account would I raise a hand if the fray rose, not though I was martyred for it. He smiled and said that was as I pleased.

We helped the boy Wattie with the gear down the windstair, for the armoury lay in the old keep hard by the barnekin gate through which they were wont to bring in the kye in time of peril. Wattie brought also the horses and ass, and told us it was done secretly, all the household being gotten indoors with the weather that had become foul as the day wore. This pleased Waitabout, in such haste as he was to begone. Not so I, liking all less and less by the minute, not only for my own base fear of my skin, but for the harm that such mad work might bring upon my lady whose thoughtless enterprise it was. Again I besought that we go in to her (in truth thinking that she might stay me) and he, all bustling as he bound the gear upon the ass, asked would I have her give him her scarf to bear as a favour on his lance point? At this I grew angry, from my fear and misgiving and

79

to be thus pushed on, but he minded me not and told Wattie to keep close until we were well gone, so that if they came to question him it would be too late to let us. But this the churl would not consent to.

"I's gan wi' thee," says he. "I can stand wi' ye at Triermain, aye, against the Nixons or a'body! Ye'll never leave us, man!"

I bade him go in and keep to his place, but he shook his head and vowed he would go, "for service to Lady Madge". Waitabout told him that here was no work for him, and he would but peril himself to no purpose, but the clown stood fast and swore he would follow if we left him. "I can strike a stroke!" cries he. "I told Lady Madge, and she never said us nay! I can strike a stroke, sitha!"

"Why, fool," I told him, "here shall be no strokes, God willing, but a show of force against thieves. And thou'rt a kitchen knave, go to!"

"And thoo's a priest!" cries the saucy villain, and fell to begging Waitabout, who seeing no help for it, told him he might go, and Wattie skipped and cracked his fingers, to my great sadness, to see a poor fool so eager to be in harm's way.

Now with the day wearing down the wind rose, with a great storm of sleety rain, so that we were soaked to the skin before ever we had mounted, and I bitterly repenting that I had given my word to go, fearing that which waited and wetter than any fish. But now it was past mending, and Waitabout bade Wattie set wide the barnekin gate for we had tarried long enough. Which he did, and then gave a great cry, and looking I saw that one stood at the corner of the peel and it was my lady, all in a great cloak and hood and her shoon sorrily wet in the puddles. I went to her, and she asked what I did there, and on my telling her that I must with Waitabout to Triermain to make all plain to the Bells, she said it was well, and thanked me for my care of her interest. This was less than I had looked for, hoping she might give up her design, or at least forbid my going. She looked to Waitabout sitting his mare by the gate with his lance across his thigh, and seemed about to speak, but said nothing, and he too spake no word. I went to him and said, would he not speak to the lady, but he would not, although they looked on each other, and again I felt that knowing between them.

So I blessed her, without giving thought thereto, and she gave no sign but still looked on Waitabout. At this I left her, and went out the gate, sorely troubled, and when I looked back she had gone in. I asked Waitabout why he had not spoke to her, and he answered that the bargain being made between them there was no more to say "and we were ower close under the chestayne tree for my liking, father, so I would not stay."

"That is an ill thought," says I. "She has given you her word."

"Aye," says he, "but a woman's word is kept after her own fashion, and it may not be yours or mine."

I had indignation at this poor esteem of her, as it seemed to me, and asked him what manner of woman he thought she was. He was silent a moment, and then said he knew not, yet, but of two things he was sure, "that she will have her way in all things, for one, and for the other, she is a right lewd lady."

Hearing this, I could not speak at first, and when I could, would have rebuked him for his vileness of thought and word, but he put in his heels and cantered away

through the rain, and not a word more would he speak
save to Wat, who called to him to mend his pace to that
of the ass. Which he did, and a slow faring we made of
it through the dank fields all misty, myself in anger to
have heard my lady so scandalously spoken of by one
that was no better than an outcast thief and blasphemous
jester, and with a chill to my marrow that was not only
of the cold rain and snell wind.

E CAME TO TRIERMAIN as the day went down in chilly mist, with such storm of wind and rain that I might have been as dry up to my neck in Caldew flood, and wished myself any otherwhere than here. Waitabout rode ahead to make circuit of the place, spying out, as I supposed, how the Nixons might come. He pricked all about, here and there, marking how the land lay, and then came in with us, cursing at the wet and saying it was no defensible place, but must serve as it would. I asked how did he purpose to front the Nixons, and he said shortly let us see what manner of folk were these Bells, and he would tell me.

Now this Triermain is a poor place enough, lying under a fair wood on a little hill, of a dozen cabins such as the borderers build, but no blockhouses like those of Tynedale or Redesdale, where they build strongly of logs. Here was but wattle and plank and thatch, although there was wood aplenty to build better, but they were a shiftless people, and as for a barnekin wall or means of defence, there was none, they having dwelt secure in my old lord's day and grown to that sloth that safety and good lordship ever breed in such folk. They numbered not above two score, a dozen being men grown, and the rest women and old folk and a great swarm of bairns that played in the mire about the cabins and in the poor plots, chasing the hens and clarting themselves, nor minded the rain.

They came out in a tribe to gape at us, and a sorry pack they were, the menfolk stout enough but dirty and ill-clad, and the women as slatternly as ever I saw, and if there were three pairs of shoon among them it was enough, and not a bonnet save that on the head of George Bell that was their chief, and it was but a piece of felt with a string under his chin. The fellows gave way to let him through, they standing sullen, but the women made a great cackle, snatching up their snottery halflings and shrinking back among the cabins to see Waitabout in his gear with lance and steel cap, as though he were a Nixon come to spoil them. He for his part held back nor spoke, looking to me to lay it open to the people.

This I did, on Bell asking me with respect what I did there, for I had not been to Triermain above twice in seventeen year, the folk being of the new faith (so far as they had any) and I under injunction of my old lord not to meddle with them; so they looked on me askance until I told them that I came to lay my lady's commands upon them, when George Bell gave a great crow and cried to them:

"Said I not so? She has a care of us, aye, aye, a good lady, a sweet lady lord! Did I not tell you she promised our security against all thieves? Oh, a sweet lady!" And asked me when the men would come.

"What men, fellow?" I asked him.

"Why, the lusty troopers," says he grinning. "To fight the Scotch knaves, hey-hey! Is't the Bewcastle watch, or Warden riders frae Carel? Aye, said I not so, they will be here anon! Secure, says she, and good guard for us and our gear! Oh, a kind lady!"

I saw that he had translated my lady's promise into troops of horse in the telling to his people, no doubt to puff himself in their eyes as one who had prevailed with her, for he was a windy reed, this Bell, and no cripple of his tongue, which I doubt not was how he had become superior among these clowns, as babblers will. I told him straight there were no troopers, but good arms for their defence, and at this his jaw dropped to his belly and he fell to yammering and bleating that my lady had promised such and such (as I think he had told his folk), and now they were left defenceless against the wolves, and no help, but all betrayed, and no fault of his, with much striking of his breast and caterwauling and excusing of himself, which the folk minded not but still looked to me.

I bade him hold his peace and harken, "for my lady has sent you a stout captain, Master Noble here, to direct you how to set your place in defence, and arm yourselves in such wise for a show that the Nixons will let you alone. For seeing you bold, and ready to resist, they will give back."

"Give back?" cries Bell, weeping. "Nay, they will take and burn all! They'll have us, harrow and alas, we are lost souls! What says my lady? She promised, she made oath, oh, Father Lewis, we are undone, all together, our wives and bairns and all!"

He ran among them bleating and crying, and some women there were took up his lament, but for the men they marked him not, having doubtless heard him before, but still stood sullen looking on us. Waitabout said naught, but leaned upon his crupper. I bade him speak to them, but still said no word, and George Bell changed his tune to cry who was this reiverly fellow, that they should heed him. Still Waitabout was silent, but presently drew his poniard, and fell to playing with it, tossing it up most dexterous, and ever higher, and span it so that it lighted hilt first on his palm and stood up and balanced there, which was wonderful to see. The men laughed, and one fellow said he knew the trick of that.

"Let me see," quo' Waitabout, and cast the poniard to him, who caught it and essayed the same trick well enough, though not so featly as Waitabout.

"Where learned ye that?" says Waitabout, and the fellow grinned askance at his billies, and said thereabouts or other. Waitabout asked his name, and the fellow said he was Janet's Richie's Adam.

"And a Bell?" says Waitabout. "So art Adam Bell, as in the old story, who was a stout man. Keep the poniard, Adam, for thou'rt my privado* henceforth. Now, had we but a William Cloudsley to bend a bow for us, we were three good men."

At this another said that he could bend a bow, and Waitabout bade him take one from the ass's back, for it was his own. "My lady wills that every man should arm himself, and keep the arms he takes, as a gift from her, to show her love for her people. Good gear, lads, and plenty on't, of lances and swords and caps – no small gifts, sista, blades of twenty shillings and more. Go on, man, find a cap to fit thee, 'tis her ladyship's bounty."

This was cunning, for the gear was such as would have cost them six months rent, and even George Bell came forward, leavening his plaints with a cry that he must

* comrade

86

have back and breast, being chief among them. He would have had a caliver, but Waitabout whispered to him that a bow befitted him better. "Good shafts, Geordie," says he, "ash wood every one, and dropped feathers. Fenny goose, Geordie, mark 'em. Man, ye could hit Carel Cross frae the Castle wi' shafts like them!" So he wheedled, leaning on his crupper, while the silly folk stripped the ass of its gear, and put on the caps and grinned before the women and bairns, that cried hey to see them, for they strutted back and forth like so many tatty Tamerlains, with the young ones making to touch the blades and drawing back all a-squeal. Thus the crafty knave armed Triermain before they well knew what he was about, eyeing them narrowly to see what of them were used to manage weapons, as Adam Bell and the fellow who had called for a bow, whose name was Charlie, and one or two likely others. And when George Bell, having made a great bustle with the women strapping on a cuirass for him, bethought him what this arming must mean, and was like to set up howl and complaint again, Waitabout bade him think what he did, that kept my lady's chaplain (as he styled me) out in the rain, and no good welcome.

"Do you go in, please you, father, with Master Bell," says he. "Belike he has confident news which you should hear, also you may make known to him my lady's pleasure, while I see to things here." I saw that he wished George Bell away, being one that would make bother of anything and hinder his proceeding, so I suffered myself to be conducted into the best of the cabins, which was a stinking pit, with a fire on the floor, and more bairns about than fleas, crawling in the corner, for they breed like rabbits these folk. Howbeit the women were at pains

87

to do for me, though somewhat in awe, and sat me on a stool close to the fire, which I was glad of for all its foul reek, for I was starving cold.

George Bell, that was full of himself, called for water and a clout to wash me, which I did, and rated the women to give me good cheer of the best they had. And this I will say, that if the Triermains lived like swine in some sort, for a filthier hovel I never was in, yet they fed as well as any of their like in the south country, aye, and better. It was but a bare board and a cracked dish with them, but they had big broth, without barley, but prunes, and salmon potched with greens, and a powdered beef that would have made a lord sing, for I never tasted better, and good bread. With it was strong black ale which they call Cumberland yell, and afterwards cheese and apples. I had a great stomach to it all, and the old grandsire that sat by the wall called in a cracked voice for them to give me hot water* also, and presently hoists up with many a sigh, and comes to my shoulder leaning on his stick and whispered that I should bless them presently "for though the folk are badly fallen hereabout, yet some of us would say Mass still, did my lady but will, aye, would we."

Now all would have been pleasant, with a full belly and the fire, but for George Bell that clattered on this and that of my lady, and how she had looked, and spoke with him, and had answered the Land Sergeant, all this being to make himself great among the women that served us, but from their looks it skilled not.

"A good lady, aye, a sweet lady, that used me kindly, and asked how I did," cries he. "Aye, and called me

* spirits

88

'Master Bell', did she not, father? And her so gowned wi' fine stuff, aye, and jewels, and gave me her hand to kiss! D'ye hear, Meg? Eh, what say, Meg, gave me her hand, oh dainty, aye, a white hand. What say, Meg?"

Meg answered that he talked as the geese muck, everywhere, and he fell to cursing her, and begged my pardon for it, but prated on of my lady, standing by the fire in his steel cap and cuirass still, toasting his backside that peeped out of his rent breeches, a very scarecrow in his borrowed gear that wist not how he looked.

Now, whether 'twas the warm or the fare or the hot water, I know not, but the fear I had felt was something diminished, having seen the readiness with which the Triermains had armed themselves, and doubting not that Waitabout would put them in such stance as would fright the Nixons. Presently he came in, and to my questions said it was well enough, for the wind had died and the mist come down, which might hinder the Nixons or cause them wait for another time.

"So should all be well, since my lady may to Carel tomorrow, and if her bright eyes prevail not on my Lord Scroop for a parcel of horse as a plump watch to Triermain hereafter, then I'm out of reckoning," says he. "Master Carleton may say her nay for his own policy's sake, but not my keen Lord Scroop, for that is one that fears not Liddesdale, not he; nay, he'll put himself in the road of any thief, Scotch or English, and take joy in't. A hard lad, a rough rider, this Scroop."

This put more heart in me, as promising security for the future, for if the Lord Warden himself gave her assurance for a day or two, she might levy such force of her own as should guard her bounds thereafter.

"Aye," says Waitabout, "but these fine things are not

for tonight, and I would it were mistier towards the Waste, so should Ill Will bide by his ingle. There is a moon in the hind-night; God send it shine not well for Liddesdale."

I went to the door and looked, and it was deep dark, and misty even among the cabins, which cheered me. I asked Waitabout what order he had taken with the Triermain men, and he said, enough. I asked, if the Nixons came, would he make a bold front to them in the village or in the field beyond where they would come, and he smiled and asked me what care I would have for the souls of the people after this.

"As to that, it is for my lady," says I. "If she gives me leave I'll go among them, as I have not done heretofore because of my old lord's prohibition. Yet I fear she will let me."

"Even so," says he. "For the care of their souls, you must wait and see, but one way or t'other, it is your charge. The care of their bodies is mine, and I too must wait and see. Each to his trade, father."

This putting off pleased me little, but hoping to see what his dispositions were, I went with him as he walked out by, going round the village, but no one about, they being gotten to sleep already, save one fellow that stood by the pen in which they had brought the cattle for safety. It was but a little herd, and poor beasts, thin with winter, that made me wonder that it should be worth the Nixons' while to raise blackmail of such a place.

"Five pound is five pound," says Waitabout, "and twenty-five in Scotland, seest thou. Nay, but Ill Will looks further on, to Langholm races, where he may cock his bonnet and say 'Aye, lads, the Dacre folk pay me black rent. What, the new lady is a wise wench, a canny lass.' That will be his boast – and if Triermain pays, then it will be Naworth next, and Hethersgill, and Walton, and even down to Brampton. It hangs on this one night, father." Saying which he smiled, and as we walked I saw him cast his eyes about, as though he looked for that which I could not see. I asked him where the men were, and he said lightly that they would come to his whistle at need.

To the north end, beyond the cabins, two fires burned low on the field edge, and I asked should they not be damped, "for if the Nixons coming in the mist should see them, they will be guided, but if they are out, they may lose their way in the murk."

"Liddesdales could find their way through the blackest deep of Hell," says he. "Nay, father, 'tis not fear of straying will keep Ill Will at hame, but if he puts his nose out of his bastel and feels the chill and discomfort. Our best guard this night will be a wanton wench and a quart of French wine in Riccarton, to keep the wolf in's lair. If it sorts with your priestliness, pray that Ill Will gives himself to fleshly pleasure even now, so are we more like to be spared."

Now it was so dark and the mist growing thicker that we could not see the wooded hill hard by the village, and for the fields the fog rolled over them like sea waves. Northward all was hid beyond a furlong distant, and all very still, save for the cattle that grunted in their pen. Being clammy and somewhat tired, I said we should be glad of Askerton the morrow, and our own beds, and did he not think that we might come untroubled through the night, "which will be glad news to my lady, if they come not."

"Aye," says he. "If they come not."

On that I left him, for he purposed not sleep, and went myself to lie down in the cabin, which I was loth to do for the vermin there, but my eyes were so heavy I might not wake. All were abed save the grandsire that sat still against the wall and mumbled, for the woman Meg and George Bell lay behind a curtain, and the lesser women and bairns on their straws and the hounds by them. I found a place less filthy, and got me down, but was so sorrily bitten, and Bell snoring like a bullock, and the stink so vile of the little Bells, and the fire reek, that I had but poor repose on the hard ground, and my sciatica no help. The ancient coughed sore and whined to himself on an old ballad (which is their great delight) of a war-lock lord that dwelt in Hermitage and so offended his neighbours that they lapped him in a great sheet of lead and boiled him in a pot.

> They cooked him on the Nine Stane Rig
> And a grand broth they made on't,
> And had his gear and beasts awa'
> His good wife and his daughters twa,
> Hey, 'twas salt tae the broth they made on't.

God save us, these are their lullabies! He was quiet at last, save for the rheum in his lungs that coughed and crackled all night long, and then I slept also, wishing I might dream of Mexico or Africa or anywhere so I was shot of this beastly border. But as our fears will make up our dreams, so I dreamed of Askerton Hall ablaze and cast down, and my lady apart on her palfrey with a hawk on her wrist that was an eagle for size, and when she cast it flew screaming "A red bull!" in human tones and lighted on a great chestayne tree where one hung, but I could not see his face that was hooded. She rode beneath the tree and looked on the hanged man, and again I felt that knowing that was between her and Wait-about, but whether 'twas he that hung I could not tell. But the hawk cried again, and the words were those that he had sung in the armoury, to wit, that a Dacre never ran away. A fell dream from which I woke slowly in a great sweat, seeing Askerton whole again, and the folk there in good attire, and my lady passing among them all smiles, with a goodly company armed to attend her, and of one side she showed a sweet smile like an angel and t'other that fell cruel smile, but the folk marked neither but pressed about her to bless her name, and so I came full waking in that clammy den, and the loon Wattie by me, urgent to russle me by the arm.

"Up, father! Father Lewis! Come awa', father, come awa'! Up, man! They's coming! They's coming!" And ran out and in again, bidding me haste that was not well awake, and in such confusion that I knew not where I was for a time, or what he meant. I stumbled out, sore lamed with the sciatica from that hard lying, and at the door Adam Bell who closed it as I passed through and set his back against it. He had on jack and steel cap and lance, and bade me on where Waitabout stood armed between the fires at the village end. Wattie bustled me on, in great alarm, although the cabins slept still, and a Triermain man armed at each door as it seemed to guard them. Yet when we were come up to Waitabout, and I all out of breath looked back, the men were gone, save for Adam that followed at pace. All was still though not so dark now in the hind-night, and the mist thinner that hung in wraiths upon the fields.

Waitabout stood with a little lad beside him, that

hooted like an owl as we came up, two or three times. Waitabout smiled on him and said he looked to see feathers and two great eyes on the child, for sure he was a hoolet indeed.

"So perch by the hanging stone," says he, "and let me hear ye when they come in eyeshot, and twice again as they pass. Awa', good lad!"

I asked him what it meant, and he said we should see anon, and bade Wattie and Adam build up the fires that had burned low, which they did, "for the moon serves us poorly in the mist, father, so we must have moons of our own to see by."

"What need of light?" cries I. "Are the Nixons come indeed? What will you do? Where are they?" For to the north was but the misty field, and no sight or sound. He answered not, but lay down on the wet ground, putting by his steel cap that he might set his ear on the turves, bidding us all be still. So we waited in the silence while the fires burned higher, and myself in a great dread what time he listened and then sat up, and leaned his elbows on his knees.

"An embassy cometh from Scotland," says he, "but I doubt King Jamy sent it. Five riders, not a mile hence. Now God damn Ill Will Nixon, and Fingerless Will that got him! Brisk up the fire, Wattie boy, and get you to your station! Bide the whistle, Adam! To it, and bid Charlie dry his fingers!"

I cried out in terror what was to do, and he stood up and clapped his bonnet on his head, signing me to be still.

"What, man?" cries I, "are they come indeed? Now, Mary help us!"

"Mary and ye will, and all other saints," says he, "but

I had rather six Robsons or Grahams to my back than all the names in your calendar, father. Yet we shall do, aye, we shall do. Now, bide you with me, and never a cheep if you would look on my lady's face again."

Which saying he drew me in to the side of the cabin nearest, and behind a cart that lay there, where we might look out beyond the fires to the meadow ground. The fires were burning high, and cast light all around, but never a man in sight among the cabins, and all as still as the grave save for the crackling firebrands. I asked him what it meant, "for will ye not post your men up in plain sight, that these thieves will see them in their gear?"

"In good time," says he. "They are but five, by God's mercy; I had feared half a score. So lie we like mice till we have them in view – whisht, there it is!"

I heard an owl hoot out in the mist, which was the little lad that Waitabout had posted out before. Then silent all, and my mouth was dry with fear as I looked on the wreathing mist, and in a moment sounds therein, as soft hooves on the turf, and a jingling of harness, and a hoarse voice that sang some doggerel and laughed thereon, and of a sudden a great rough voice that called: "Geordie Bell! Are ye waking, Geordie man? Come aff your wife and oot your bed, ye bugger!" And more of the sort, ribald cries and laughter that came ever nearer through the mist. And the owl hooted twice.

Waitabout took me by the arm and whispered. "Ye've seen devils painted, father? Now look to see them in the flesh, for this is their hour, half past midnight to dawn and their foray before them. Now, not a word or a sigh. Lie close, and wait. Aye, and watch – and remember!"

It needed not the caution, for I could not have stirred

or spoken for my terror, to see presently dark shapes in the mist that were of mounted men, swollen to giant size by some trick of the fire glow in the murk. They came slowly on into clear view and halted beyond the fires, and I was like to swoon as I looked on them, for never had I beheld night reivers or the terror of them, that are but men by day, yet from the dark they are goblins from the nethermost pit. All five they sat in line on their hobblers, in their jacks of black leather and steel caps above, and I might not make out their faces 'neath the skips which made them the more terrible, silent fell shapes without feature as they were. They spake among themselves, and then one cried out for George Bell to come out and kneel before them, and lay his black mail at their feet. Now, I thought, Waitabout must go out to them, lest they be angered, for still they roared for Bell, and called him scab and cuckold and bastard and such foulness as I would have stopped my ears had I dared to move. But he was quiet yet at my shoulder, nor moved, and then the five came on again, slowly, bawling and cursing for George Bell to come out or it should be the worse for him.

"Tarry, will ye, by God!" bawls one that was foremost, a hulking fellow and old, for I saw his beard white above his jack. "Tarry on me, ye bastard, and ye'll roast on your own fire! Come oot, and your clowns with ye! Hobbie – see's a brand frae the fire yonder, and we'll light the bastard afoot wi' his own thatch!"

One of them rode to the fire, and stooping took up a flaming brand from the fire. I heard Waitabout by me hiss through his teeth "Light down, light down!" and as though to command he of the beard dismounted and another with him, and came on, leading their beasts, and the three riding behind, of whom one sprang from the saddle.

"Three afoot, 'twill do!" says Waitabout, and whistled on a sharp note, whereon the five stopped, and in that instant I heard the harping of strings and the swish of shafts, and two of the five staggered and cried out, shot through with shafts, and Waitabout was over the cart with his sword in hand, crying, "On them, on them! A red bull! A red bull!" And of a sudden, where none had been a moment since, there were Triermain men that leaped from the cover of the cabin sides, with swords and lances, and rushed upon the thieves, and all crying "A red bull!" And now I saw such a sight as never I saw of slaughter and horror among Christian men, and all in a moment betwixt the fires at Triermain.

The rider with the burning brand being still ahorse, Adam Bell ran in on him with a lance and gored him a great thrust in the belly, whereof he fell on the ground, and his horse upon him. Another that was shot of the arrows fell also, and the Triermains came at him with their swords and spears, but one of the Nixons bestrode him and laid about so handily, roaring amain, that they gave back from him, crying for Charlie of the Bow, who shot upon him, two shafts, but still he fought, though on his knees, when the Triermains came to him again.

This I saw, but could make out no more for that the press was so thick, with men striking and cursing and all in disorder what time the steel clashed and rang on helm and jack, but Waitabout I saw, yelling like a very devil with sword and dagger, and Adam at handstrokes with him of the beard that had an arrow in his arm, and the loon Wattie with a lance also, crying out like one mad. I stood stricken by the cart for the horror of it, having looked to see some parley or truce beforehand, and not this fray of ambush, and indeed I cried out which brought a Liddesdale down on me that burst from the fight all torn and bloody of face and made at me with an axe, to ding me down. The boy Wattie came between and was like to have taken the stroke had not I, never thinking, run and gripped me the Nixon by the arm, in the which doing I took a dint of my left breast that I thought had broken it in, and a grievous cut to my arm, for he swashed me such a stroke as was like to take off limb and all. I fell swooning for the very pain of it and was trampled on until one dragged me from the press and the hellish clash of arms, so that I lay clear but all wet with blood mine own and others, and everywhere was blood and screaming to heaven and vile cursing and worrying like hounds, and my senses left me as they fought betwixt the fires at Triermain.

How long I lay a-swoon I know not, but not long I think, for when I came to myself there was still clash of steel and shrieking terrible to hear, and the boy Wattie knelt by me as I lay against a tree that grew by the cabin nearest the fire. He had torn away my shirt, and the woman Meg made shift to clean my hurt arm with a hot clout, and I was aware of Triermain men before me that dragged upon a rope, and saw above my head one that kicked and struggled hanging, and there were shafts in his body, and blood fell about and some on my face, and George Bell dancing and cursing what time he thrust at the hanged man with a lance. So more blood spilled and ran down upon me until the Triermains, seeing this, bade Bell desist, which he was loth to do, but ran where was another Nixon held between men of the village, and a shaft in his breast also.

"Hang him up!" cries George Bell. "Give him his own Jeddart justice! Fyle his bill! Fyle his bill! Oh! Oh! Oh! Up, lads, up!"

One cried that the Nixon was dead, but Bell said it was all one, he should hang by the heels, and they put a cord about his ankles and swung him beside his fellow, and gored him with their spears and knives also, and he ran blood like a collander.

All this I saw in a maze, not understanding what I saw, but my senses coming to me again I would have cried to them to let be, but my tongue failed me for the pain of my wounds. Waitabout came and asked me how I did, and looked to my hurt that was himself wounded with a gash to his forearm. I said I did but poorly, and bade him make them leave off their horrid slaughter on the Nixons, but to this he made no answer. I commanded him again, but weakly, and know not in what words, but something of bearing them to Carlisle for justice, and he looked up from binding a moss upon his wound and looked on those two that swung grisly above.

"How carry them?" says he. "And if I could, what's the bill? Blackmail, of which they would ride free upon assurance, and so to harry again! Let be, father. Triermain is safe this night, seest thou."

Now I saw that he looked not on me, but beyond, and turning saw the other Nixons held and bound by the people, and the women clawing at them, and they sore hurt and all besmirched in blood and mire, and they were three, the old stout fellow, and two others. The old man they beat and slashed at with sticks, and the women tore his white beard in bloody tufts, and he never left off bellowing lustily and cursing them. Another they took by arms and legs and held him spreadeagled against a cabin, and tore off his clothes, all naked as he was, and George Bell struck him in his face and cursed and railed at him, and fell to pricking his belly with a pitchfork, again and again, so that the blood ran down, and the fellow prayed for his life to those people that raved against him like not men but beasts, for they glared and laughed demented and the women like witches. George Bell thrust the fork into his belly, and others the same with knives and swords so that his bowels fell out, yet he lived and cried to heaven, but they had no pity of him but thrust his hands through with knives and left him crucified. And all this I saw, but could not be heard for their shouting and cursing.

Now Waitabout went to the prisoner that was by the bearded man, and took him away from the Triermains, though they cried he should not, and cast the fellow down by me, and said they should not have him, and to my wonder said that he was now under the arm of the Kirk. At this they grumbled but let him be, and the Nixon, that was a stripling but right hard of face, had his hands bound and bled of his wounds. He cursed them, and then presently asked was I a priest. I though almost shent with my wounds and the beastly sight of all, answered as best might that I was.

"And I John Nixon, that they call Hungry Jock," says he. "Now do thy duty upon me, priest, for 'tis my time this road. Hear my sins and assoil me, and that quickly, and mind I am that Hungry Jock called Patie's Jock also, and not Hungry Jock o' Stobs my cousin. Father, forgive me for I have sinned . . ."

And I heard him as in a nightmare, his face close to mine, and such a tale of horror he told, of four great murthers, and above twenty women other men's wives that he had lain with in Scotland and England both, and of thefts and woundings and oppressions and iniquities that galled my soul to listen. I asked did he repent, and he cried by God that he did, and would sin no more, for the Triermains would see to it, and begged that in absolving him I would give separate absolution to his right hand, for it of all his members had been left out when they baptised him so that it might strike unblessed blows upon his enemies in feud – and this, as God sees me, is also the custom of the country!

There was great commotion about the bearded Nixon, him that was the leader and called Ill Will, and they tugged him all ways, some saying he should hang and others for having at him with their blades, and Waitabout stood by watching but silent. The old man, that was a very spectre what with blood and mire, besought them for his life and cried "Blackmail nae mair!" and swore to let them be, but they dragged him to the great dunghill that lay beside the cattle pen, and there heaved him up, and drave him down head foremost into the filth, and held him there, and all the trunk of him within the dunghill what time they held his legs. They laughed and cried to him to eat his fill of Triermain, and presently his legs gave over kicking for he was drowned in the dung, and naught but his feet to be seen. And ever Hungry Jock pattered his sins in my ear, and the Triermains men and women, aye, and even the bairns, danced ring-around the dunghill, sneezing and laughing and fell down all.

Perchance I swooned again, but I know not, for thereafter was a time of voices crying, and George Bell to the fore, and Hungry Jock taken from where he lay, and I cried out for them to spare him being so moved by their horrid cruelty that I babbled of cursing and excommunication, but Waitabout came to me and said I should have content, for all was done. And looking, I saw that the four corpses of the Nixons slain were laid all in a row, and headless, which blasted my sight to see, and with ropes about their feet they hung up all four in the one tree, and Waitabout bade Hungry Jock look well upon them.

"Tell Liddesdale," says he, and bade them bring a reiver's hobbler, which done they hove up Hungry Jock to the saddle, for his hands were bound behind him. Then came George Bell and another bearing a leather sack leaking blood, and well I knew what gear was therein, the heads of the men slain. Waitabout made it fast to the saddle-bow.

"This for the widows and mothers of Riccarton," says he, "from the Lady Margaret Dacre. Thus she pays her blackmail."

Hungry Jock looked upon him, but spake no word, and then upon me to whom he said, "God keep you, father," and bade Waitabout put the bridle 'twixt his teeth his hands being bound (such skilly horsemen they are). The Triermains in a great ring about watched him silent, and he put in his heels and rode away betwixt the fires at Triermain.

HEY BARE ME into the cabin that might not stand for dizziness and pain of my wound, where an old wife gave me hot water to drink and for my arm that stung me so sore I swooned again, and so lay between waking and swooning while she sewed up the wound right cunningly and bound over a poultice of moss. Looking to the dint on my breast she probed with her fingers so that I near wept for the hurt of it, but said I would do, and gave to Wat a bag of moss damp saying my wound should be bound with new moss daily to make it whole, which it did, healing in time to a great scaur. So, I say, for a wound give me an old village wife that knows her simples over any doctor of London that would have purged my bowels and cupped me to death, aye, Lopez or any of them. My breast is coloured with a bruise that aches now and then to this day, but my arm is whole and pains me never, for which I thank the good leeching of the old wife of Triermain, though it smarted a week after.

She had work that night, what with men that had taken hurts (though none so great as mine), what with one Jenny Bell that came to her time when the fray rose, and was delivered of a fine boy that grat loud to be heard in Cockermouth, a lusty lad. They in the cabin where I

lay, a great press, bickered what he should be called
other than Archie, which his grandam would have in
honour of Waitabout that had saved all, some saying he
should be Archie Four Knaves in memory of that night,
and others Archie Rise-to-the-fray for that he had come
forth roaring timely to the onset. I heard all this but
partly, to my disgust that they should load a child with
names of blood and strife, and bade them leave off their
vile calling, at which they were abashed and the grandam
bade me peace for they would think of a proper name at
their more leisure. Which they did, and God help me he
is called Archie a-Blackmail.

Now think not that I make much of petty things, as
my wounds and a bairn's eke-name, which I but noted
at the time, for I was overweighed with sorrow and anger
for the horrid slaughter that had been done of no necessity, aye, between the fires at Triermain, that shall haunt
me to my last sleep. I would have spoken of it when
Waitabout came in to me, asking how I did, and with
him George Bell that brayed his triumph as though he
had won another Pinkie or Solway Moss and himself a
very Hector in his steel bonnet and tattered breeks, calling off the names of the slain, as Ill Will and Half-
drowned Geordie and Clem the Clash and Ringan's Hob,
with great jeers at Liddesdale that had gat its bane that
night. For all my faintness I would have cried him down,
but Waitabout cross-talked over me, saying I must be
quiet for my hurts, and aside to Bell that I was feverish
and should be left alone. Which abated his glee a little,
though still he cried of four dead that had been great
thieves, and what should they say now on the Scotch
side, "hey-hey, what say Adam, will they talk o' this
in Branksome and Hermitage and Ferniehurst, how we

fettled the Nixons at Candlemass, what say, Adam, hey, how now, Charlie lad, did we not fettle 'em, hey-hey, what say, brave lads?" And clapped Waitabout on the shoulder familiarly as to a brother-in-arms, "what a captain, hey, what a man to a fray, what say, did we not gi' them auld gruel between us, thou and I, hey?" that himself had made more noise than action and slain a Nixon while others held him, out of fell cruelty, and gored the corpses with his fork.

I would have cried out on him for a beast and sinner, but again Waitabout came between saying I must for my health back to Askerton straight, and bade Bell and those there make a litter to convey me that might not ride. And all but Wattie being gone out, Waitabout looked on me and sighed and bade me speak my mind to him if I listed, "for I see ye must for lease of what is within you, but as quietly as ye may, I beseech you, lest ye grow fevered."

I demanded why it had been done so bloodily, without remonstrance or parley or any show of arms to fright the Nixons, but by ambush whereby were four men dead unshriven that might have lived, and the weight of murder on his soul and the Bells. He answered shortly that there was no other way but suddenly, "for ye saw these Nixons, what manner of fit men they were, and mounted, and give them a yard of law or advantage, they would have ridden Triermain through and put the Bells to the sword, aye, had they been fifty to the Nixons five. Wi' such as Ill Will's band to parley is to submit or die; ye must strike first and unaware, or ye strike not at all."

This, he said, had been his purpose from the outset, but had not told me for fear I would have tried to prevent him, "and had the Bells seen us at difference, there had been no doing anything with them, to bring them to fight."

I said he had deceived me wickedly, but ambush or no, could they not have been taken whole, or with slight hurt, for justice, "but ye slaughtered wantonly, making a carnage that need not!" He answered that the Bells being hot and raging that had suffered at the hands of thieves in days bygone, and in great fear besides, had been past preventing. This I said was a lie, for he being commander might have stayed their hands, and should, "for my lady bade thee protect her folk, not welter her village in blood!"

"And will ye instruct me, father, out of your vasty knowledge of arms, how to do one without the other?" says he. "Nay, forgive me, but I teach not you how to pray! And if I could ha' taken them gently, and with little scathe, would ye have had them spared to ride on Triermain another day?"

Aye truly, said I, spared for their souls' sake, and those of the Bells that had butchered them like brute beasts, and for his soul, and mine own that he had made me party to the deed.

"Because ye grappled a Nixon in the fray?" cries he, and laughed. "Is that where the shoe galls? What, man, it was bravely done, and kept the life o' the loon that sits by you even now! Wouldst have him dead rather? Nay, go to! As for the slain, father, they lie not in your charge, unless ye take on you my sins and the Bells, aye, or the sins of all the world!"

Between grief and pain I cried out did I not bear the sins of every man, did not he, did not we all, and was it not for this Our Lord died?

He said he truly believed Christ died that had no

choice, being taken of His foes, nor had died for our sins that had not yet been sinned. "But I see I have angered you, though whether for slaying of the Nixons or for disturbing your spirit, I cannot tell. And if your soul smarts for this night's work I find it passing strange. Is your mind's peace of greater account than the lives of the Triermain folk? Are the Nixons to be let live and slaughter and rob for the ease of your soul and mine? Nay, Christ taught not that, surely!"

Seeing him grown hot, I put away mine own anger and besought him as best could in my sorry condition, that knew not what he said, to seek God's pardon for what was done, to which he answered impatiently that if I meant, to confess, it was a sham, "for what is confession but telling God what He knows already? For is He not everywhere, and if He marks the sparrow's fall shall He not mark Ill Will that went head first into the dunghill? Let be, father, He knows me and you – aye, and my lady – and all that has passed this night, aye, and were ye by Ill Will's grave would ye not comfort the widow that it was His will? So fret not for my soul."

I wept, being sore of my wound and the torment of his wild words, at which he laid a hand gently on me, and begged say no more, and hold my peace before the Bells, "for it would be unseasonable chat in such an hour, when their stomachs are high for their own manhoods and the security of their wives and bairns and gear, and little like to fret of the Nixons their souls. So let be, father, and if you will, turn your plaint against me presently, but let the Bells alone, for your talk will do naught for the keeping of Triermain at present, and that is my charge."

I gave over, more for my infirmity than his entreaty, and presently was aware of a brown comely girl of the

Bells that stood by the door and smiled on Waitabout, who frowned and signed her away yet went presently and spoke with her, and coming again to me bade me rest and Wattie should bide and keep the folk from me, and then went out after her.

Wattie, that had been by all this while, was quiet, but then sighing, asked me timidly was it wrong that he had fought withal, and feared he had hurt one of the Nixons, "for I fetched him a mighty ding that wounded you, and another I thrust at but did him but little harm," and rambled on of the same, how he had been angered and rejoiced for the Nixons slain, for which he was now sorry, and was it a great sin, surely, and Papist though I was could I but make all straight he would be beholden to me, and what should he do, and what of Hellfire? Babble of this kind which, to my shame, I heeded little, but bade him say his prayers and we should talk at a better time, for I was come to such faintness and distress corporal and spiritual that I could but lie there half-waking in my pain.

After a time came Waitabout again, and Adam Bell that gave me his shoulder to the door, and they put a cloth litter between two beasts and myself therein, and Waitabout mounted the one beast with cap and lance and Wattie the other. Now did the Bells clamour about us, a few calling for my blessing but the most for Waitabout, laughing and weeping and crying "God thank you!" and "A red bull!", and the brown girl I had marked before stood at his knee and held his hand, smiling wantonly, which grieved me sick to think what they had been at and the blood not yet dry betwixt the fires at Triermain.

George Bell would fain have companied us to Askerton, thinking to strut before my lady, but Waitabout said he must bide there with his folk by my lady's command, "but presently you shall come in to her, or she out to you, for be sure she shall know how stoutly the surname Bells of Triermain have borne themselves this night." George Bell was downcast, and said it was not fit being chief man that he should not go in to her, but the woman Meg fetched him a skelp to his lug that knocked off his steel cap, bidding him peace, and Waitabout would none to come in but the little lad of the owl's hoot, to bear a link to light our way, for it was yet full dark.

So we came away from Triermain that I have not seen since and would I never had done, and my wound throbbing a great pain, yet no such pain as was in my spirit. We fared wetly through the fields and ash woods, and as it drew light Waitabout gave me to drink hot water but a sip, which something revived me, and we fared on, but with no talk between us.

Now as we came a mile nigh to Askerton we were aware of some that came towards us in the misty dim of dawn, and foremost Yarrow the deputy bidding us in a great voice stand. We wondered to see him who (I learned anon) riding on some affair in the hind-night, and chancing by our house, had learned from the bailiff of Waitabout's watch to Triermain, and made great to-do thereon, and Lightfoot the lawyer waking also at his books had heard them, and been in great alarm, wherefore all three were come out, which was a great folly to my mind, for what could they do to any purpose? The bailiff was but part sober and laughing, and Master Lightfoot lapped about in a great coat and shawls aboard a mule, sore sneezing and wiping his neb red with the cold, and Yarrow cried out what of Triermain. The

Waitabout reported what had passed, and all three sat as men stricken by a spell, but Yarrow most of all. For when Hodgson exclaimed of the four Nixons slain, crying "By Hell! By Hell! Saints be wi' us, what a stroke here! Who wad credit it?" Yarrow swore, not he, for one, and put it to Waitabout that he lied, "what a scabby rascal, thou, and pack o' daft clowns the Bells, to pull down four stark Liddesdale men? Away, thou rush, go to!"

Waitabout bade him ride to Triermain and see for himself, at which Yarrow cried out again that he lied, and all three babbled in amaze until Yarrow coming by my litter and seeing me wounded was like to fall from his saddle for astonishment, and I told him it was true. He went black with anger, willing not to believe it even now, and for the bailiff he bellowed his admiration, crying "Four stark Nixons! Ill Will and a'? Hey-hey, the Waitabout! Sic a night's work! D'ye hear, Master Lawyer? What, Anton, what say?" and taking Waitabout by the hand, who said it was no such great matter to put down a foe that had his belly full of pride, "for see thou, the Nixons thought to find sheep, but found men, fifteen to their five, and so had their faring."

Master Lightfoot, when the lout that led his mule had holpen him down, to great cries of "Stay, knave, stand so, lest I fall!" and gathered his shawls about him and ascertained of Waitabout and myself that it was true indeed, groaned and went white even to the nose of him. He shook and was silent biting his finger, but of a sudden broke out that he must inquire of this fully that had fallen out on my lady's ground, "as to wit, attack and assault and grievous hurt and slaying, within her demesne, which if it should fall to be answered at law, we must be clear of all blame, and my lady's innocence appear that was no party thereto any way, aye, shall appear, aye, shall it so", all in a great pattering of words what time the Waitabout leaned on his saddle-bow and looked on him with that crooked smile.

The bailiff cried the lawyer to leave it, for here was no matter of law, but demanded anxiously were any beasts lost, or goods of my lady's tenants, or houses burned or spoiled or any such damage, as to dykes and fences and farm tackle, "aye, damage, man, see thou, aught that will cost?" Waitabout answered that a few of the Bells had taken scratches, but no harm done to beasts or village or insight, to which Hodgson cried it was no matter for scratches so the gear was safe, "for the buggers would make a pound damage out of a broken pot, see thou, and seek stay of rent for it, would they not, aye, George Bell would he!"

He was in a sweat to be home with the news to my lady, she being abed still, but Master Lightfoot laid hold on him, saying time enough for that, it must be thought upon, aye, and in no haste, whispering in the bailiff's ear, who looked askance now on Waitabout, and presently Master Lightfoot said he must have word with him on the instant, before we came to the house, so Waitabout got him down, and the lawyer taking him familiarly by the arm drew him aside in close talk, and very earnest with him, while the bailiff cursed the rain.

Myself was content to lie in the litter, rain or no, being faint but spared for the moment the uneven motion of carrying which had distressed my wound. As we waited, cold and wet enough, the bailiff and the deputy fell to brangling, for Yarrow being overcome with the news knew not whether to go, stand, or anything, while Hodgson seeing his vexation, and guessing it came of jealousy of the Waitabout, jeered slyly at him, and said, had he but had the wit, when my lady besought his aid and Carleton's, he might have offered his service, and had the glory that was now Archie Noble's. "And him but a broken man, but you, that could not see Skiddaw till it fell atop o' thee, why, ye had your fortune in your hand and saw it not!"

Yarrow damned him roundly, asking how, and the bailiff said had he served her (and she a close marrow of the Queen's Grace), then surely his fortune had been made out of her gratitude, that had stood her champion in her sore need. Yarrow swore he could not, being bound by his commission and Carleton's command, on which the bailiff brayed a great scorn.

"A fig for Carleton and thy commission that between them will never get thee but ten score shilling a year and a lance in your liver! Why, man, wouldst ha' won the favour o' Lady Madge Dacre, and where would that not ha' ta'en thee, aye, to office and preferment and the Court even?" He smiled behind his hand, saying my lady might have wed him even, her saviour and a proper man, and the simpleton deputy, not seeing himself mocked, cried out in wonder, on which Hodgson, savouring his ill jest, spoke of one Lacklugs Armstrong, a man of no account on the Scotch side, that had yet married a knight's widow with a thousand pound a year, and he that had no beard or shoulders such as Yarrow's, and cast-eyed to boot.

Yarrow gnawed at his nails to hear him, and still Hodgson plagued him, that had lost not only a fortune but credit, "for ye might ha' ruffled it round Carel Cross the day, and told the boys o' four stark Nixons slain, and how Ill Will was bad to handle but ye fettled him at the last wi' your swashing stroke, your backhand lick, so, beneath the oxter, aye, and killed them a' yoursel', bar one, and bade them excuse ye to Lord Scroop, and would ha' cracked a cup wi' him, but ye must back to Askerton where Lady Madge stayed supper for ye, aye, fowl and green lettuce and a grand claret. Aye, Anton lad, what might ha' been, but you, your brain's in your pintle, honest man!"

At this the poor deputy saw the game, and was like to choke for rage, and said let Waitabout look to himself how he would answer for the work, "for he'll no thanks of the Land Sergeant or Wardens, nor your fine Lady Nose-i'-the-air, neither!" Looking to where Waitabout and Master Lightfoot conferred, he muttered of taking him up to Carlisle straight, and Hodgson laughed and cried, aye-aye! take him up that slew the Nixons, belike he would ride meek to Carlisle!

Yarrow bit his lip and said he would ride first to Triermain, to see if it were true indeed, and Hodgson bit his thumb at him and the Land Sergeant and Warden also, saying it lay not in their charge that had washed their hands of Triermain yesterday, but the red bull could mind the red bull's business, and let that content them. And as Yarrow rode, bade him beware the beasts nibbled him not, so green he was.

He then inquired of me my wound at last, and again questioned closely that no harm had come to Triermain its cattle or furniture, of which I reassured him, and he was satisfied, saying it should be great comfort to my lady that the Nixons were put down, as also that the cattle and beasts were secure and the Bells with roofs to their heads, and her rents safe that way. "What! A great stroke, aye! And if 'twas more than we looked for, what o' that? Oh, Tom Carleton, what shall ye say to this? What o' thy quiet policy now? Aye, or Liddesdale or the whole border? Hey-hey, a little bit lass not a day in't parish, and snaps her fingers and whist! four great thieves laid stiffer than the Pope's conscience! By, man, a feather in Dacre's hat, this!"

I doubted she would so regard it, and yet wondered what she might make of it. For in short space had I seen how each weighed the thing in his own fashion, the bailiff counting in goods and gear and rents assured, the poor callant Yarrow in jealousy and hurt pride, Master Lightfoot in terms of law and good appearance, doubtless the Land Sergeant according to his policy, even the boy Wattie in fear of his soul, but none in lives lost, and souls also, save my poor self. I said somewhat of this to Hodgson, and he answered, aye, father, each to his trade, seest thou.

Now Master Lightfoot, that had stood apart rattling like a windmill at Waitabout's ear while we endured the bitter weather, came and said we should in to Askerton "and there take order how to proceed, for it were well to be prepared beforehand against any point of law, though none shall rise, I think, yet Justice loveth a careful client, so shall we consider well, to make all straight." And sneezed and sneezed again, and told Waitabout he should have content, but leave it in his hands awhile, all should come right, good fellow, aye, right enough. And now inquired, with much shaking and sneezing, for my wound, and said it must be looked to, aye, a sore wound, though not got through any fault of my lady's, but accidentally, yet sore enough for all that and must be tended presently, and more of the like until the bailiff, that ran with rain like a pump, cried on him to leave drivelling and mount his ass before we drowned there in the fields. Which he did yet babbling, and Hodgson chafing after him, and Waitabout looked on me right wearily but said no word. So we came again to Askerton Hall as day broke.

Y LADY BEING NOT RISEN Hodgson would have sent word through her maid to apprise her of Triermain, but this Master Lightfoot would not have, saying she might hear anon but first there was much to be done, so let her be, and for the household the less said the better, "for gossip maketh mischief, and it were well no foolish rumour or light talk were bruited about." The bailiff said stoutly she must be advised straight, whereon Master Lightfoot, that was commonly an aye-nay-mayhap sort of man, became peremptory, saying he must have his way for my lady's sake, whose man of law he was and did but for her good in matters that the bailiff knew not. They would have fallen quarrelling had not Waitabout taken the lawyer's part, and bade the bailiff heed him that knew his business best, "and we were beholden to you rather for dry clothes and a bite to eat, and some medicine to our hurts that have borne the brunt of it this night." Whereon the bailiff gave over, though sullenly and with many shrugs and ill looks to be thwarted of telling my lady which he would have done with great advantage.

He would have had me taken up to my bed, but Wait-about, having looked to my wound and taken my pulse, said I would fare better in the warm, so they put me in the hall, in a little privy corner or nook in the wall by the fire, such as the Spaniards call an alcoba, with a bed therein and screen, where my old lord was wont to lie after deep drinking that he could not manage the stairs to his chamber. I was glad enough of it having shed my sodden garments, and my teeth chattering as with an ague, but Wattie made a great fire of which I had the benefit in my corner, and Hodgson gave me a posset hot and spiced that I was the better for, though weary and sore in every limb of me.

Waitabout stripped him before the fire, bidding Wattie do likewise, and now we saw that the lad had taken a sore gash to his leg in the fray, but had said naught of it. Waitabout cuffed him gently, calling him stark man and mad wag that minded not the knocks he took, and washed and bound it for him. "So we are three with patched wounds," said he, "the priest and the loon and the broken man, and all got in the fray at Triermain," and said they should make a ballad on us of "we three", which liked me little enough that had borne an unwilling part therein. They two partook of beef and a mess of eggs, but I had no stomach to it, but only the hot dram of posset.

So was I like to have slept from my great weariness, but did not, for in the hour that followed I heard and saw that which kept me waking, aye, as wakeful as in the fray, for it was as fatal withal, though never a blow struck or hand raised, and gave more grief to my spirit than all that had gone before, and abideth with me still and ever shall.

Master Lightfoot being gone about his affairs, and we three alone in the hall, came the bailiff bidding Wattie to bed, and Waitabout also for whom there was a place prepared in the armoury, "a right bed chamber for a man-at-arms", says Hodgson heartily, and clapped him on the shoulder saying he had earned his rest, aye, and four-fold for the Nixons, and had my old lord been there he had given him feathers to lie on for his good service.

Waitabout thanked him, but said he was for the road, having naught to stay for, and would be away on the moment. I marvelled at this, and the bailiff also that gaped and then laughed, clapping him again and saying he should by no means leave so suddenly, "and thou but half-fed and sleepless, go to! Nay, man, for our credit and thy good shalt bide at ease in Askerton a twelvemonth an ye list, for my lady would not have it other! Also she will look to hear from thee of Triermain, and do thee service in turn."

Waitabout said she would hear of it well enough, and for himself he had better away, "for the bargain's kept, and the day risen, nor am I comfortable indoors, for myself and others." He looked on me a moment smiling, and asked was it not so, "for you, Father Lewis, have had little comfort of me, and Master Lightfoot even less, and for my lady who can tell?"

Now at this my heart smote me, for though he had much angered me, and given me grief on his behalf and mine own, yet I would not be the cause of his going off so poorly requited, that had done good service in his fashion, which if cruel and beastly to his foes yet had he perilled his life and kept Triermain secure, and this on his word given that he need not have kept being wrung from him on fatal compulsion by my lady. He might have fled away, yet had done his devoir, as they say, and I was loth to see him depart without notice.

So I said he should stay for my part, and I doubted not for my lady's also, and the bailiff swore it was a daft start, surely, for "but wait you upon my lady's coming down, I warrant there'll be a pound or two for thee in this, aye, good money, man, think on!"

Waitabout laughed and said there had been no talk of more fee than the door open and a clear road over the fell, "and so that I keep the steel bonnet and sword it is enough, master bailiff, that and Black Dod's hobbler at the barnekin gate."

Seeing him resolved against all persuasion, the bailiff said he would see to the horse, but it was a folly, for sure my lady would reward him if he stayed. Hodgson being gone, I said as much again, and bade Waitabout bethink it were scant courtesy to my lady to be away without a word. He smiled awry, and said she would excuse it, and for courtesy between them hers had been of a hempen kind when last he saw her, and he knew not what her present humour might be. I cried shame that he should doubt her, "for whatsoever means she used to compel your service, yet now 'tis done she will be beholden to you, and do you good besides."

He took up the steel cap and weighed it in his hand, still with that narrow smile, and said he doubted I had dwelt overlong among peasants, "for gentlefolk are not like them, Father Lewis, as King Saul doth witness. No, nor lawyers. Necessity called last night, but if I read Master Lightfoot aright, Prudence is the counsellor now, and Amen to that."

I asked what Lightfoot had said to him in the fields, and he said he had asked exact account of what befell at Triermain, and even more jealously of the bargain made with my lady beforehand. "Now a nod's as good's a wink, father, and I think he would not have me tarry at Askerton, but reasons that if mischief should follow of last night's work, haply if I go I may carry it with me." And asked me smiling did I not know that when a deed was done past recall, those who had willed it were wont to think little kindness of the doer, though they had set him on. "They cannot be shot of it, but they can be shot of him, so let him saddle and ride."

I said he did my lady wrong to think so meanly of her, and he answered it was all one, for he would go, but first would take leave of Wattie, "for that's one of good metal, aye, dirty but stout beneath, and deserves well of you and me." Then said he would return presently for my blessing, "if it please you give it to an unworthy offender, for his comfort, and it may be for your own."

So I lay alone in the hall a little time, and my thoughts busy as the crackling fire, heavy at heart that he should go, for there was that in this same Waitabout that I would have known more of, and being gone would leave an emptiness behind that would not be filled thereafter. I knew not well why it should be so, and know not now, save that he was such as one doth meet but rarely in this life, having their eyes open upon the world, subtle men whose faults are many and their errors great, yet are they uncorrupted in their hearts, seeing as children, simply, so that at all shifts and trials and hazards there is but one word for them, and that word is "true".

And as I lay drowsing, I heard a foot that tarried on the stair beyond the door, and two voices that spake as in conference, the one in question and the other full of busy instruction, and knew them for my lady and Master Lightfoot. He as ever talked at a great rate full earnestly, but more softly than his wont which I was hard put to make out, for I thought no shame to play the eavesdropper, I assure you, being greatly curious, and if it were wrong I brazen out the fault gladly.

He was urgent with much wordy vehemence that she bore no blame for what had passed at Triermain, "for mark it well, this Waitabout Noble slew these same Nixons, he and the Bells at his direction, and had no licence or permission from your ladyship for this, who bound him only defend your village and make it secure. So are you clear there, if it should come to any bill or charge or claim for damage or compensation for their deaths, as might arise, though I think it shall not, but yet it might."

I heard my lady answer doubtfully that she had plighted her word to answer for Waitabout what he did, to which Lightfoot cried, aye, indeed, "but this was on your handfast bargain only, which I think shall not hold at law, being only the custom of the country and short of a proper bond, to which the priest and bailiff can testify that were there when 'twas made. So, at law, no blame may lie against your grace for aught that followed therefrom, you being not lawfully bound."

At this she gave a good round trooper's oath. "Blame? How can blame lie, on our side? These thieves, slain untimely, were spoilers in arms that came to assail and bleed my tenants, and by God shall I not defend mine own?"

"There you have it, lady!" cries Lightfoot. "Defend's the word, and this you set him to do, but not to slay over-barbarously as he did and bade others do! For thus it was, as I conclude from what I have learned of the fray from your lout Wattie, aye, and from this Waitabout himself. For resistance and security, well, but murder is another word, and this it might be called before the Wardens. But of this you stand clear, content you, for that your bargain with him was not lawful in any case."

Here he gave over, for now they were come into the hall, and my lady frowning in perplexity, yet when she saw me where I lay in my nook beyond the fire, cried out and hastened to me. I saw she had waked to the news but lately, having on a mighty fine gown of shotten silk over her night rail with dainty broidered slippers to her feet, and her hair unbound which was a wonder to see so long and flaxen fair, falling either side her shoulders nigh to her waist and there was clasped with a cingle of silver links such as I never saw the like before. She was lily pale in her looks, as well she might be on such tidings unexpected.

"Master Lightfoot has told me of your hurt," says she, "and would to God I had kept you home, for I would not have you take harm in my behalf for all the world!" And took my hand right tenderly when I made shift to rise, staying me, and smiled and said naught should lack for my comfort, and would have a chirurgeon from Carlisle to see to me. I was abashed but right glad to see her so moved on my behalf, and could have borne more of it, but Master Lightfoot croaking at me was Waitabout gone yet, and I answering that he bided, he stamped and muttered in his beard, and drew my lady away with more anxious advice, that she should remove to her chamber until the fellow was safely gone.

"For it were best you saw him not, for if it should be known that you had speech with him after the fact, why, this might be seen as approving him, and might by shrewd advocacy appear as a conference or conspiracy between you, if it should come to law, so please you my lady withdraw, and I shall give him such discharge as shall content him, and your ladyship shot of him."

Now this was such dealing as Waitabout had foreseen, aye, to the very words, that I was amazed, and knowing my lady's proud stomach, thought to hear her bid Lightfoot go hang, for she would speak with Waitabout if she so willed. But she frowned, as one in doubt, and ere she might speak I heard Waitabout whistle without, and then he was come in, and stopped in the doorway at sight of my lady. Then Lightfoot put his back to him quickly, and looked on my lady with such a face of boding as would have frighted sheep, and whispered urgently to her that she say not a word, nor so much as a look, but to mark him not at all, and presently withdraw.

Now Lightfoot left her and came to Waitabout with a great false smile, and took him by the shoulder to lead him by the farther wall to the window with "How now, good fellow, what, not away yet?", walking wide of my lady and not looking upon her, and babbled at Waitabout that it was well enough he had tarried departing, yet he might be gone soon enough when he had heard somewhat to his advantage. And ever Lightfoot kept himself between Waitabout and my lady, as though she had not been there, which to my mind was the vainest pretence, but who knows the minds of lawyers?

My lady being close by me, I saw she liked it not, as contrary to her own desire and wont, yet unwilling to run against her own advocate his counsel who had been so earnest with her, and indeed it is a foolish client that doth so. But for her very pride she would not withdraw, but looking neither right nor left went to her great chair that stood across the fire from where I lay, and there sat with a set countenance.

Lightfoot asked Waitabout, was he a lettered man (knowing well he was), and Waitabout, having looked to where my lady sat that marked him not, put on his droll face and said he could make shift to write "but in the accent of Bewcastle only, the rude phrases of Northumberland being beyond me, though I can read them and a little Scots too." Which answer confounded the lawyer that knew not the fanciful rogue he dealt with, but he passed it over and came to his point, that there was no written bond with my lady for what was done at Triermain, "but a handfast bargain, aye, in good faith, but an understanding only, ha?"

Waitabout looked long on my lady turned away, and set his shoulder at ease to the wall, and said, even so, a bargain that she would answer for him, and what o' that?

Being a lawyer, and this his meat and drink, Master Lightfoot told him what of it, with fine windy periods at length as one useth who is loth to speak plain, as commonly ariseth when the letter of the law is so-and-so but the spirit of it must be breached wide enough for a battery train to pass through. The marrow of it was that Waitabout having wrought great slaughter at Triermain, which my lady had not foreseen nor could countenance, and his service having been engaged not by lawful bond but on handfast only, it might be that if any claim or charge arose, that she could not well maintain him at law, or answer for him, howsoever much she might wish so to do. For she was greatly beholden to him, and wished him right well, so for convenience it might be best if he gat himself out of the March speedily, for then if complaint arose there would be none to answer it, she being under no obligation, and Waitabout not being there, "so, how say, good fellow, all will be right, go to, ha?"

For my part, I never heard a sorrier sophistry, and had Ananias been above ground he had cried quits with Master Lightfoot that hummed and hecked and span his words by hook or crook to prove my lady clear and hoodwink a simple broken man (as he thought him). And all this while my lady sat like a statue that frowned troubled but spake not, and Waitabout looked curiously upon her at a distance, and no longer with a droll face.

Lightfoot now fumbled in his scrip and gave Waitabout a paper, saying that if his road lay through Penrith he should show it to Master Lowther that was a lawyer of the town "who will give you that shall ease your passage away, for 'twere best no fee passed in this house, nor are no names named in the paper, but a line only to requite the bearer, that I think shall content you."

Waitabout looked not on the paper but still on my lady silent, and told Lightfoot no fee was needful "nor all your persuasion neither, for had ye not held me in chat I had been past Brampton by this. Nay, sir, it needed not you to make it plain that I am unwanted here, having served my turn, and the peril being past Askerton would fain see the back o' me."

This in a light pleasant voice that my lady heard full well, for I saw the crimson mount from her bosom to her cheek like a tide, and her hands grip the chair. A moment she sat ere she came to her feet bright-eyed, and if the boy Wattie had grovelled there with his logs I warrant he would have taken such a kick as would have carried him to Bewcastle Cross. Master Lightfoot, his back being turned to her, saw not this but rubbed his hands and smiled, praising Waitabout his quick understanding, but said he should take the paper that well deserved it. Waitabout shook his head, but said there was something he yet would have, and the lawyer in quick alarm asked what it was.

"Why," says Waitabout, "I think 'tis for my lady to say."

Hearing this she turned to him, high of colour and taking breath to command herself for wrath against him that spoke the reproof and against Lightfoot that had been the cause of it. He looked all distraught from one to the other, and was like to trip on his gown in agitation to prevent her answering, clocking like an old hen that if Waitabout would say his desire, it should be through himself, "such being my lady's pleasure, nor is it meet she should speak you," but he had as well tried to dam Eden with his shoe, for she snapped at him to hold his tongue, "for shall I not speak to my servant?" He waved his hands and would have prated on, but she cast him a look that stopped him dumb, and with a little crook of her finger bade Waitabout come to her.

He stood before her with not two yards between them, and she with her head high asked what he would of her.

"Not this," says he, and stooping put Lightfoot's paper on the fire, at which the colour left her face and by and by there grew there the ill smile she had worn in her hanging humour. "What then, fellow?" says she, and January wind had sounded kinder. "Is it too little for thee?"

He answered that, much or little, it was by the way, "for as I told your man there, 'twas not in our bargain, which was that I should serve and your ladyship maintain, an obligation both ways. Well, I have served, and if as your counsellor makes plain I am not to have the maintenance promised, well, it is no matter, for I need it not, looking to be out of the March this day and beyond all plaint or charge. So you are quit there. And yet," said he, "there is a little thing that I would have, of no sterling value, but counted high in the custom of this country."

Now I trembled as I lay there, doubting if the high and potent Lady Dacre had ever been spoke in such wise before, in courteous rebuke of her plighted honour, and this from a broken fellow of no esteem that disdained her maintenance yet with all respect. She could not well believe her ears, and would fain have boxed his for insolence but her dignity prevented, keeping her countenance but with a Gorgon eye, and I marked how her hand gripped the stuff of her gown like to tear it. She asked him with a hard eye, what was the little thing he would have?

He said it would leave her no poorer, "though me it shall enrich greatly, unless Master Lightfoot find another loophole to deny me. Nay, my lady, 'tis but this, at parting: a word of thanks."

Now was she at a loss that I had never thought to see out of countenance, as myself and Lightfoot, who had looked to hear him ask some thing material, however small. I marvelled that he should goad her so that was right dangerous to meddle with, as he knew, yet the rogue did it full craftily, in all humility and spread his hands.

"Nay, lady, 'tis little enough to ask, surely. What, for your village secured, and the Bells kept in health and goods, at peril of my life – aye, and four great Scotch thieves laid stark, two gored and slashed like mincemeat, one drowned in the dunghill, another unbowelled wi' a pitchfork, and their four heads sent back to Liddesdale in a bag?"

"I asked not that!" cried she, and thereon let blaze at him with such a fury as made my old lord's choler seem but a whisper, for she stamped her foot and damned him for a brute beast that dared flout his barbarousness in her face that she had never looked for nor could countenance, but when she drew breath he spake gently as before.

"Do me right, lady, did ye think I went to play at pat-a-cake wi' them? I served you as best I knew, aye, and better than ye know, for I secured not only Triermain last night, but Askerton and all your folk and lands for ten year hence! Oh, believe me," said he in all earnestness, "they will ride wide of you hereafter. For even now they look aghast on those four heads and whisper 'Christ Saviour, what a woman is this!' Nay, noble lady, if ye doubt me, ask Father Lewis there, or your lawyer, or your bailiff. But I beseech you humbly, reproach not me for my zeal in your service. If it was over-zealous, as you and the priest do think, well, the fault is all mine. But the benefit is all your own, for you have your safety with a clean conscience."

Whether he mocked or not I could no way be sure, and am not still, though my lady with her keen wit suspected it, yet looking on his face so comely open that met her eye soberly, knew not how to answer, and being wroth with herself therefore, sat herself down with her gallows face again, and baleful bonny she was.

"Ye will read my conscience to me, will you, master reiver! Well, I tell you it was beastly and bloodily done, and I am to thank you for it? Nay, I should thank you with an iron through that ready tongue of yours, by God!"

"For telling truth, lady?" said he, and shook his head.

"Nay, you are too honest for that. For truth it is, and if I put it bluntly or was over-bold to show you how peace and safety are secured, faith, it is right you should know these things for what they are. It may be a hard lesson here, in your quiet hall, but had ye been at Triermain ye had learned it first-hand. And barbarous or no, I think ye would not wish Ill Will's head back on his shoulders." Looking on me he said: "Though Father Lewis would, which is a wonder, since his own Jesuits do hold that the end doth justify the means, and if my means were foul yet shall the end be fair for Dacre and Askerton."

Had we been solus, he and I, I had spoken my mind of him and the Jesuits both, but ventured not now, waiting another thunderstorm from my lady, and if it came not pat yet did I fear its gathering, for her eye was angry bright and her nether lip doom itself. A long moment she sat regarding him, and God forbid she should ever so look on me, or that I should deserve it for so speaking her plain like a schoolmaster in patient instruction of a wilful pupil. But her mind was at work, though I read it not, and sure it was as shrewd as his, yet how she would have answered God knows, had not Master Lightfoot, who through this had been like a mouse on a hot griddle, railed forth of a sudden at Waitabout, rebuking him roundly that dared beard my lady with such scandalous familiarity and loathly talk of bleeding and bowelling, and called him rogue and thing and malapert common knave and a dozen lawyerly terms besides. At which my lady turned her wrath on him, damning his intrusion, "and if you could state a case as simply as doth he, ye would have had a woolsack to your arse long since!"

Being the better for that venting her anger, she turned

again to Waitabout, sitting back in her great chair and eyeing him right coldly.

"Well, sirrah, you look to read me a lesson, and yet methinks you are at great pains to excuse yourself, but let that be. For your boldness to my face ye deserve the whipping I forgave you yesterday, but since I judge boldness to be the best part of you, I let it be again. Nor shall I debate ends and means with you, for I see you are one that thinks no small beer of his oratory, and I'll not humour you there." And now she stood up, and I marvelled to see her frosty look gone away, and in its stead a little smile as crooked as any of his. "This only shall I say, that for the slaughter ye wrought let your own conscience answer whether 'twas needful or no. I did not look for it nor will condone it. But for that ye made my folk safe, and served me bravely in my need, I thank you with all my heart and ever shall."

Hearing this so unlooked for I marvelled again at the shifting minds of women that will be hot one minute and the next cold, or go from mirth to weeping and back in the blink of an eye. Though in her this changing was outward only, and within her will was ever steadfast, for good or ill. She spake it with a pretty pride, and right nobly as became her, and I thought that whatever good might come to Waitabout in his life, never would he have better than those words of hers. It took him unaware to get the thanks he had asked for, but having it he bowed his head and answered her right well.

"Now God thank you, lady, that was courteously said, and more than I deserve for my frowardness." He begged her pardon for that, and I would he had left it there and gone away with all good will between them, so should much evil have been avoided, not least to me that have carried the weight of it these many years. But either in kindness to her or to pay Master Lightfoot for his dishonest dealing, he said that in amend for his blunt speech to her he would lighten her mind of a burden that the lawyer had put there "in telling your grace that you had cause to fear action at law, or bill or charge for what I did in your name at Triermain. Heed it not, lady, which was lawyer's moonshine that knows not the custom of the country. There shall be no plaint against you out of Scotland, nor ever could be. What, a riding surname to cry redress at law for hurt taken by their blackmail reivers in the open doing of their crime? Nay, that is not their way. Even Ill Will would laugh if he yet had chops to grin withal! You may bid Master Lightfoot back to school, or to Hampshire!"

Lightfoot shook to his dewlap to be so rallied by one he had termed rogue and thing and malapert, and his weighty opinion set at naught, but my lady having taken him by the ears once he was loth to vex her again, so held his peace. But she, who saw ever to the point, asked Waitabout, if no plaint or charge was to be feared, what need had he of haste to begone out of the March? He put it by, saying he was so minded that tarried not long anywhere, but she suspecting some better reason, pressed him, and so he must satisfy her.

Truly, he said, it was for his own skin's sake, "for though there shall come no legal plaint out of Scotland, be sure there shall come lances, and after one quarry. There is Hungry Jock Nixon that sits this while in Calfhill Tower telling such a tale as will make Flodden seem a petty bickering, and word of the tokens he bore runs even now from Caerlaverock to the Merse. Aye, and one name with it, and that name 'Waitabout'. Nay, lady,

Hungry Jock will have my head on his point if it take him twenty year, he and his kin, and that means half Liddesdale, what of Elliots, Crosers, Armstrongs and a'. They call it feud, seest thou, and they are hundreds, stark vengers all, and I but one broken man, so must I be done wi' this frontier right early, and shall never see it more."

At this she cried out and looked to Lightfoot, who chittered and shook like an asp-leaf, with wringing of hands and Godamercy we are all undone forever, and oh, had my lady but sought his counsel beforehand, but Waitabout laughed and bade him peace, "for as I told you, they will ride not on you or Askerton, firstly for fear that my lady would pay them again as they were paid at Triermain, having great riches and power to levy arms, and secondly because it was I alone that was red hand in the deed doing. So me they must have, for their honour's sake, and for the four empty saddles. Nay, they would think shame to look for revenge on any here but Archie Noble Wait-about-him. But his head will content them."

This was a wonder to my lady, who sought first my eye and then Lightfoot's and so back to him in her astonishment.

"And ye told me but a moment since you had no need of my maintenance? Now, by God's wounds, I never saw one that needed it more!" And rounded again on the lawyer that had told her naught of this, "but quibbled and twisted me with your words whether I should or should not maintain the man at law, and how for convenience 'twere best I were shot of him, cozening me to neglect my bond, but never a word that his life lay in the hazard, why, thou prating beetle, thou!"

Master Lightfoot was like to weep, protesting he had not known, whereon she tongue-lashed him the harder that had counselled her in ignorance, "aye, and would have had me break faith, thou clementine mouldy gargoyle, what with your might and should and mayhap, thou gaberdine canker! Shall I not stand by him that stood by me?" And seeing Waitabout smile, cried did he dare grin at her, and should she not keep her word? At which he grinned indeed.

"Now there spoke Dacre, there bellowed the red bull! Nay, sweet lady, never frown on me, for though you honour me with your concern, yet truly there is no need you should secure me. For I am weary o' the border, and right glad to go, nor shall their vengeance come up wi' me this side York, and beyond that they cannot ride."

Now this talk between them had been plain and straight and well understood by both, and by us that marked it, the lawyer and myself. He was troubled to hear my lady so hot to maintain the man, come what might, but I was pleased to see such worthy intent in her, and good feeling between them. But now there came a change upon them, and I doubt that Master Lightfoot divined it for all his subtlety and sharpness, for it had naught to do with practic matters outward, but was of their inner minds and regard each of other, being man and woman. For now my lady looked on Waitabout with a difference, which I think had been in her heart these many hours past, but only now did she make it plain to him, speaking right proudly.

"And how if it is my good pleasure to secure you, aye, and right potently? How if I undertake to maintain you here 'gainst all comers?"

He asked, to what end, "for if you give me assurance

under your lordship, then shall the feud encompass you and all yours, and, lady, while I value myself well enough, I am not worth a border war, and that would be on your hands surely, for their honour's sake."

"What you are worth is for me to judge," said she, and a little wanton quirk touched her lip and was gone. "How if I make you my constable of Askerton land, to raise and lead me troops of men sufficient to any peril from Scotland? Was it not done lately by my grandsire, and sure if you can make these great thieves, these Nixons, hop headless with but a sorry parcel of clowns to back you, can do the like for all the Scotch border, given but power thereto." And now she smiled indeed, but right pridefully as became the Lady Dacre. "What lacks to this? There is gold enough, God knoweth, so shall there be no want of men or arms or good maintenance. Well, Master Noble? How if I offer you this?"

This was a marvel to me, though for Lightfoot he would have been gladder to see Clement's Inn afire. The Waitabout kept his countenance before her challenge that had in it such esteem of her station, but not that only. For in that moment there was again that knowing between them that I had seen afore, and now it went to the souls of them, and if any say a priest can be no judge of such, I say that a priest is a man still and knoweth as well as any the way of a maid with his kind. Waitabout knew, for I saw his face, that here she made offer not only of place and fortune, but of her own self, and, light mind that I have, I heard in mine ear the bailiff's taunt anent one Lacklugs that wed a knight's widow, and Waitabout's own word that had esteemed her "a right lewd lady", he having seen in her that wilful humour that recked not of consequence so it met with her own desires.

What had wrought on her, the great lady, that she should fix upon the broken man, I know not, though indeed he was a stalwart lad comely enough to look upon and no common man, but wrought it had, and but for my presence and the lawyer's I doubt not she had been more forward with him still, and what might have come of that, who knows, not I.

So she stood, proud as the Queen's own self, bold of eye and lip and sure in her beauty fair. He spoke soberly as though in awe, which well he might be, saying here was more than ever he had looked for, "yet bethink your grace that if ye make me your constable and chief at arms, ye throw down a glove that Liddesdale shall snatch up, aye, and mayhap more than they. Ye will shake loose the border."

"Do I care for that, so I keep my word to my own liking?" said she, with a fine disdain, and if her brow was pale her glance was warm enough. "So, Master Noble, ye have had time to draw breath and settle your wits. How if I offer you this," and made a little spit in her hand, and held it forth, "and more besides?"

Even Master Lightfoot knew, with those three words, whither she went, for he turned green and wrung his hands and gazed on her and Waitabout as though they had been basilisks. Myself was spellbound and all forgot my hurts, looking to see him take the hand held out in such sure confidence, and indeed he regarded it, and then herself, but shook his head.

"Indeed to be my lady's constable and man were great honour, and beyond my deserving, and so I thank you, but it may not be."

She was like one turned to stone for disbelief, and then she cried wherefore? in a hard voice that shook. He looked down, his head of one side, and sighed, and then threw up his head and begged her pardon, "for I would give no offence to such a fair offering. But there is a chestayne tree beyond the barnekin, and it casts a long shadow."

It smote her like a blow, and she went white to the lips for astonishment, gazing on him wide-eyed until her colour mounted, and then if ever I saw a look to kill, she had it, but commanded herself. She turned straight about and sat in her great chair, her knuckle white on the boss, and though shame and hot rage were in her that had been refused so unlooked for, yet she mastered it. A long moment she sat, then rising again, spoke short.

"You have leave to go," and with that was out of the hall nor looked behind her. Master Lightfoot turned this way and that, and made to follow, and bore up dismayed, and then followed again, and Waitabout came where I lay and held out his hand.

"You must bless me in my absence, if bless me you will," said he, "for I have tarried overlong. God keep you, Father Lewis, and mend your hurt that was well got." And smiled, saying they would make a forayer of me yet. He took up sword and steel cap, bidding me tell the bailiff that he might put bread and cheese in the kitchen window thereafter for a merry remembrance, "though I come not for it, yet another may," and so was gone.

OLY CHURCH DOTH WELL to let a priest from marrying, for having no wife or child to cherish of his own, so is he fitter and more apt to love and care for all mankind, making of them his family. This is the glory of his calling, and not the least of his burthens, for when those he has cared for are withdrawn from him he hath no kin nor kith to turn to for comfort, save God and His saints, and so gets him to prayer in his loneliness. As I did now, that in truth had done naught for the souls of Waitabout and my lady, though I had great care in my heart for both, but might not show it to them or any way benefit them thereby. For one was gone I knew not whither, and without that grace I might have helped him to by persuasion, though I do doubt it having striven thereto without avail. The other I might not serve not being within the Faith, which grieved me that knew her sore of spirit, for to such as my lady pride is the very life of them, and hers had taken such a dour dint as she had not known in all her small score of years, and was like to be ill-minded therefore.

Being dejected and failing of sleep for the soreness of my wound, I got up from my couch, and saving a giddiness that passed, was well enough. Hodgson coming in to see how I did, gave me more of the posset, and I was even better. He had heard of Master Lightfoot something of Waitabout's going, and was full of scandal and wonder at his naysaying my lady's offer of service, guessing shrewdly what lay therein, "for sure I thought e'en yesterday she had a fancy to him, for all her airs, hey, father, how say ye? What, for a constable, oh, a lusty constable, hey-hey! Aye, I said but now to the lawyer, she would ha' put him to the gallows one day, and to bed the next, for had I not seen it in her eye? I did, did I! And she slept not afore three, saith her maid Susan. Aye, what o' that, father, hey? Nay, but he's best away, the lad. What? Silk lies not well against sacking, never. A month hence she would ha' been like to puke at him. Off and on, on and off, that's the way o' the gay ladies!"

Now out on thee and Lightfoot both, thinks I, for it will be the talk of the parish by supper-time, and when he marvelled that a broken man should so neglect his fortune, I bade him hold his tongue for a rank tattler that knew not what he said. He brayed his great laugh, saying what did a priest know, but there was a swift stop to his folly when my lady came down of a sudden, booted and breeched in her boy's habit for riding, pulling on her gloves and bidding him sharply to summon her page and palfrey, for she was for Triermain on the instant, and Hodgson must attend to show her the way.

"Aye, and see to your charge that should have seen to it hours since! What, a village of mine beset by thieves, and a fray and hurt done to tenants, and God knows what scathe to their goods and houses, and my bailiff takes his ease and a bellyful of beer! Aye, skip, Hodgson, you shall hear from me, Hodgson! Skip to the kitchen, where Susan gathers necessaries for the people, and have 'em packed and attend me straight! About it, man, go, go, skip and shuffle to some purpose or I'll have that log-scattering knave in thy place, and thou'lt tend the fire in his!"

She railed him from the hall, and I was as glad as astonished to see her in her busy mood again so soon, though pale she looked and somewhat hectic about the eye. She rebuked me for being up and must sit me in her great chair by the fire, and taking away the posset called for Susan to make me a rosewater drink which was sovran, she told me, against fevers from bloody hurts.

"Bide and stir not till I return," she said, "nor vex yourself for all this bother, of which you have had enough already. Nay, I have neglected you, and these poor folk of mine, what with windy talk of lawyers and the like!" And while we waited for Hodgson she paced about tapping her switch and putting sharp questions of Triermain, as what injuries had been taken, and what damage, and of the folk how many were young and babes, and how habited and housed, and sware a great oath when I told her. But of Waitabout not a word, nor you may be sure did I speak his name.

Page Peterkin coming in to say that all was ready, she snapped his cap from off his head and clapped it on her own, saying she had burned her bonnet yesterday, and did this well become her? Which it did right saucily, and looking on her so smiling fair, if pale, I was moved to think Waitabout a great fool.

When she was gone there came in Hodgson full of dole, saying she had taken a kitchen wench that knew the way "and would be of more service than I, whom she called a handless slug and a tunguts and I know not what beside! God, to be so miscalled that served my old lord three-and-twenty year, for she'll turn me out, father,

I ken fine, aye, will she! Jesus, a harpy and a vixen, and a bitch that she is! And I serve as best I know, do I not, father, did I not ever? Aye, but slug and tunguts is all my thank!"

I bade him mark her not, for she was young and peremptory and in no good humour that day, but would be more comfortable anon, when all was more settled. Nor would turn him away, whose worth was great, I assured him, and indeed it was not little to manage under command. She would not be so cruel, I said. But he was glum.

"She'd ha' hanged that broken bugger, aye, would she!" says he, shaking his chops. "Aye, though she had a right wanton fancy to him, sure she did. Will ye read women to me, father? Nay, but who can? Straws i' the wind, blaw here, blaw theer, and a pox on them a'!"

He was in and out, and I sat on by the fire, when in the mid-morn was a great bustle without, shouting and clatter of arms and horses, and Hodgson crying that he knew not and cared less, and then Master Carleton in a loud voice saying he should have care enough presently, aye, and more than he, my lady for one and that sleek ferret lawyer, too, and where was the varlet Noble?

They came, the Land Sergeant with a right February face and Yarrow at his heels, both booted and sworded for action, and Hodgson swearing he knew not of Noble that had ridden an hour past, at which Master Carleton gave him a long finger to his face and spake him roundly, "for sitha, Robin Hodgson, I will have him, with or without thy help, but better with, for thy sake!"

Hodgson cried that he could not tell what he did not know, and Master Lightfoot then coming in, the Land Sergeant breathed in his anger, and bade him and myself good morrow civilly enough, and told us his business was the instant apprehending "of a broken man Noble, called Wait-about-him, lately in this house and elsewhere in the employ of my Lady Dacre."

At this Master Lightfoot raised a great cry that to speak of employment was more than he knew for, there being no bond or contract of service in lawful form, and Hodgson besought the Land Sergeant to bethink him was there not harm enough already that he must seek more, to which Master Carleton said we knew not what harm was, yet, and asked me did I know where Waitabout was gone?

I said I knew not, and he looking on me closely, asked most peremptorily how I had come by my hurt. Now this examination irked me, as did the man himself, and I told him the question exceeded his authority, at which he laughed right bleakly and said first my lady yesterday, and now myself today, would teach him his office, but might come to rue our teaching. Then bade Yarrow put a hound on the straw in the cellar where Noble had lain "so we shall have scent of him enough, and bid Christie light the Netherstane beacon and bring word if there is answer from the Waste or South Tyne."

Hodgson and I looked wondering on each other at this, such heave and ho, what with Land Sergeant and deputy and a troop of watch at our door and bale fires (for such beacons were lighted only on great alarms) but Master Lightfoot, having ever the law and my lady's interest in mind, protested that they might not make free of her cellar, and with great dogs, too, which might be well enough for a common man's cottage, but not here without lawful leave.

Carleton showed him his teeth and said the bailiff

would give him leave, "and if it is a point of law, why, I may put a turf on my lance and call 'Hot trod!' and that, you know, shall compel any man to come with me on the pursuit. How long since ye last rode thirty mile at a gallop, master lawyer?"

That put Lightfoot's candle out soon enough, and Hodgson said he would not hinder them from the cellar, but that it was March madness to talk of trod for one poor fellow that had but served her ladyship, to which the Land Sergeant let loose his wrath.

"One poor fellow that hath hamstrung me four Nixons i' the dark, by God, and the border like to burn for it! Now, look you, master lawyer and bailiff and priest, I labour for patience, so mark me well. Here was a peaceful March, a quiet charge, give-a-bit-take-a-bit, and in one hour the policy of months is all undone by a slip of a girl that hath not been in the country long enough to fill the jordan! A masterless knave, that should have been crowbait lang syne, and shall be, by this hand, is set on by this madcap female over a nothing matter, in flat disregard o' my counsel, and by her licence butchers me four o' the first men of Liddesdale! No half-penny lifters, seest thou, but men of a name, cut up like buttered toast at a snap o' my lady's dainty fingers, God save me!"

We cried out together, Lightfoot vehement that my lady had given no licence thereto, myself that the blood was shed all against her will, and Hodgson boldly that if Carleton misliked it, he had himself to thank that bade my lady shift for herself.

The Land Sergeant threw up his hands, asking were we mad, and where our wits not to prevent her, "or had ye no thought of what might follow? Jesus, we have seen bloody war break on this border over a pair of spurs or one horse stolen, and here are four great thieves slaughtered like sheep, and their heads gone as a jeer to their kinsfolk that can have three thousand lances in the saddle in an hour, and south o' the frontier in two? My God, where is this woman, that I may look on her again?"

We said she was gone to Triermain, and I, thinking what Waitabout had certified, said we had confident advice that they would not ride on Dacre land, having had such rough handling as should put them in awe of her who ruled in Askerton. He put his brows up and arms a-kenbo and laughed at me.

"And thou a priest that says it? By God, father, ye reason like a reiver! Aye, like enough they would let her be. What then? Is Askerton the whole frontier? No, Christ's nails, nor a fiftieth part of it! And if Liddesdale, for vengeance of four namely men murdered in England, should ride red ruin elsewhere in England to slake their fury, would it content her ladyship that they left Askerton alone?"

We had naught to say, but stood mum until Hodgson asked what he would do, and the Land Sergeant cooling somewhat said it was done already, "for I have not been idle to mend the mischief done by your madcap mistress and her scabby champion. There shall be no riding on England, such as would ha' been had I not sent my messages this morn to Buccleuch and Carmichael beseeking them hold the reins, aye, and a whisper to Hungry Jock Nixon's ear, too, shall quiet him to his content. What, he is chief o' his name now!"

We were encouraged to hear him so cock sure, and Hodgson said he had done well to mend it. The Land Sergeant answered negligently that mending was his profession, and read us a weighty lesson on the balance that he and others English and Scotch kept on the border, "being at all shifts and policies and quiet dealings day in year out to keep this pot of blood from boiling over. Aye, my masters, we make and mend on a great scale that hath the Queen's Grace in one pan and the Scots King in t'other, and every borderer, lord, lady, tenant and outlaw, aye, every beast and sheaf on the beam between, and must not spill. So we come and go, and wink at small mischiefs, and if George Bell have his head broke for a penny blackmail, why, let it be."

God knows it was a sorry speech, yet I knew it true enough, though had he taken as much pains yesterday there had been much sorrow spared. Having lessoned us, he was in better humour, and said to Master Lightfoot that while for pride and meddlesome ignorance he had never known my lady's like, "yet you may advise her that Master Carleton whom she disdained and despited but yesterday, has naetheless been at labour to patch up her folly, aye, and has it all stitched but the last knot, which is called Noble."

He said this last with such fell meaning that I was afeared, and would have asked him what he purposed, but then there came one of those foolish starts that distract from all business, for the maid Susan coming in, who was a bustling shrew that cared for no one, and hearing him miscall my lady, rebuked him right tartly, and he offended threw up his chin and bade her go rattle in the kitchen. She not abashed let fly on him a fine storm of abuse, calling him Captain Sournose and a mannerless Scotch baboon, which struck him dumb a moment to be taken for a Scot, but gritted his teeth and roared at Hodgson to take out that ranting gypsy.

"Gypsy!" says she. "Gypsy, quotha, thou lying beast!

144

Gypsy in thy nasty beard, thou northling toad! Know that to the Earl of Essex I am Mistress Susan!" And there swept off, leaving him adrift and gnashing, but Master Lightfoot taking his arm quieted him with smooth words, saying he would advise my lady how well the Land Sergeant dealt, with all good will on her behalf, "and so without homily bring her to a good disposition, which shall make for amity between you."

Carleton answered him curt enough, but now there was uproar before the door, and Yarrow, that had been in the cellar, came in crying that one came with word that there was a smoke on the Black Rigg. Now at this the Land Sergeant straight forgot his sullens, clapping his hands, and stood with eyes closed while I might count to ten. Then calling for pen and ink wrote in haste, whiles instructing Yarrow.

"He is into Denton, he is fast! What, Anton, said I not his way must be 'twixt South Tyne and Gelt, for the high fells? Nay, cast about, Waitabout, this hound has your trail! Carey's men cover the Middle March bounds, and Salkeld by this should have a rider on every top from Hartleyburn to Talkin." He gave his letter to Yarrow, saying to Lord Scroop by a sure hand, "and for thyself, south wi' a hot spur, taking only two lances, Christie and Old Moffat were best, and when he is ta'en see to him yourself, and the token to Liddesdale. And, Anton, all discretion."

Yarrow cried done, and was away. The Land Sergeant stretched himself like a great cat on a wall, well satisfied, and listened pleasantly when Master Lightfoot came murmuring again that all should be well so my lady stood clear, "for sure she is untouched by all this, Master Carleton, in point of law, as I have made clear, and

145

indeed I have in mind precedents that shall content my Lord Scroop."

Carleton smiled on him and took his shoulder. "Precedents. Nay, I like the word. A bonny word, i' faith, and hath a fine hissing smack of advocacy about it. Precedents, I say!" And clapped his shoulder. "My lady is well served at law, go to. I look to our happier acquaintance, good Master Lightfoot. Now, sirs, I must to Carlisle. Health to you all, and a canny day."

He went forth in high fettle with his rapier cocked behind, but I hasted after in fear and wonder at what I had heard, and plucking him by the sleeve asked what of Noble. He tying his cloak strings said lightly, why, what o' him indeed?

I said that by his leave it were better let Waitabout alone, "for know, sir, that whatever Master Lightfoot may say of the law, truth it is that my lady bound herself to protect him from all claims or charges, and did acknowledge this in my hearing not an hour since. Now, if Master Yarrow bring him in, it may prove an ill service to her."

"Amen to that," says he, and we being now without and he by his horse, smiled at me askance and said I should fear not, "for my lady will be at no discomfort on that score or any other. Your long reiver will not trouble the March again."

Now my wits that had been dull enough before came to my aid, and I saw at last what he purposed, Yarrow being gone to receive Waitabout from his takers, and murder him as a sop to the Liddesdales, who should have his head as a token. I cried out in anguish and laid hold of his bridle as he mounted, saying he should not do this thing. He shook me off right angrily.

"Are ye mad of your wound, priest? What have I to do with murder? I shall not even see him."

Mad I was indeed, for I cried out "Murder!" again in a loud voice, saying it was an unlawful slaying without trial and he and Yarrow the Queen's officers sworn to uphold the law, at which the folk there stared to hear me, and Hodgson coming out laid hands on me bidding me give over nor meddle in what concerned me not. I shouted still and would have dragged Carleton from the saddle, but my wound letting blood I was like to faint and so fell down, crying that he could not justify it. Hodgson helped me to a place by the wall, and I still calling out Master Carleton looked on me a while and then lighted down before me.

"Father Lewis, I am at pains to do my work, and you come howling at my lug to no purpose," said he, and even in my distress I wondered to hear him so weary quiet. "Y'are not ignorant of this border. Ye know right well that whatever shifts I must be at to smooth this business, one thing skills over all. Ill Will must be paid for, and in one coin only. Thinkst thou his folk would be content wi' less, or that I shall grudge 'em, wi' the peace of the March at stake? Nay, man, be quiet and decent, for the folk look at you."

I cried out was it decent one should die without jury or priest, for serving my lady on compulsion, "and if he did more than she knew, yet were she here she would maintain him. Will ye not wait upon her? Let her speak to his guilt or innocence, if he must answer at law." He put this by with a wave of his hand, and getting to his saddle again looked on me with his long sheep face. "Law? Guilt? Innocence? Oh, sir, I have a frontier to keep."

He rode away and his varlets with him, and I wept. The bailiff helped me indoors and looking to my wound bade me be quiet, "for bubblin' will not mend Lang Archie's neck, though sorry an' a' I am for him, and yet 'tis none so hard, seest thou, father, for he'll get nae mair than he gi'ed the Nixons. What, man, 'tis the border, ding up, ding doon, knocks go both ways."

I lay nigh swooning in the great chair, and he called in the maid Susan to look to my wound, which she did right busily and well. But there was no peace, for in a moment came a great caterwauling, and this was the loon Wattie who, having heard somehow what was toward, had risen from his bed to bicker with the bailiff, and came after him into the hall. Hodgson swore at him to get gone, but Wattie gave him back curse for curse, vowing he would have the Land Sergeant's blood, and Yarrow's also, if they did harm to Waitabout. Hodgson stormed out of all patience, and the clown ran in a frenzy to the fireplace and snatched up the great iron, crying that he would do this and that upon them both though he died for it, and then his eyes started from his head, and I saw that my lady was come in unexpected from her riding, for she was still in her boy's habit and drawing off her gloves and bonnet.

Seeing Wattie with the iron raised, she told him the fire was not a cuddy that would go the better for beating, and he dropped it straight and ran to her falling on his knees and crying that they were gone to slay the big reiver (for so he ever called Waitabout) and entreating her and pawing at her boots. She bade him sternly keep his muddy hands away and get him to the kitchen, and when he was clean and in his senses she would hear him if he spoke to be understood. He weeping and crying out

148

that she must hear, she fetched him a sharp stroke of her switch to his shoulders, bidding him begone, but seeing him hobble as he went, asked what ailed him, and he stammered that it was a hurt to his leg that he had taken at Triermain.

Now at this she was all quick concern, bidding Hodgson help him to a bench, and had his wound been seen to or dressed, and did it pain, "for see, it bleeds, and what filthy clout is that to put upon it? Run, Susan, fetch hot water and a clean cloth! So, boy, be quiet and it shall be seen to!"

Wattie was in awe to find the great lady so earnest for his comfort, and hung his head to be so mothered after, and fearful too, but seeing her smile on him and call him a brave lad, would have made his plea again for Waitabout, but she frowned of a sudden, bidding him put up his face to be seen, "for foul though it be, I know it, surely! Hobbie, Johnnie, Gibbie, nay, but I have it, Wattie! Why, thou art that Wattie boy, and I knew thee not! Thou and the pony, what called you her? Aye, Daisy, pony Daisy!" She laughed, and asked did he mind the sugar plums, and what was the cordial called?

He said it was dandelion, and his face was like the noonday sun, to be so remembered by one that he esteemed nigh to worship. She snapped her fingers, crying dandelion it was, and called him boy Wattie, Wattie boy, shaking her head that he was a man grown now, and with a wound on her behalf, "and see, Susan, he is flushed o' the cheek and hot, and would be better on the couch yonder, for methinks he is distressed and feverish."

They put him on the couch where I had lain before, and I being got up from her great chair came to my lady and said indeed 'twas not for his own hurt he was distressed, but for the man Waitabout. She bade me gently back to my chair, "for indeed you look not well, and should have stayed abed, but Wattie is before you now, so must ye sit. Hey, our hall is no better than a hospital!"

Perforce I sat, and she turning to Hodgson told him there was little harm done at Triermain "save the ruin that I doubt not comes of your neglect, sirrah, and though the folk have small hurt of the fray, yet I never saw sorrier wretches in my life, and for their habitations they are sties I would not kennel a dog in at home. And that I will not have on land of mine, master bailiff, so mark me, this is your charge, and shall be seen to right soon, or ye will hear from me!"

She bade Susan bring her a cup of Spanish and water, and ere I might speak called Hodgson back again, inquiring what bedding was in the house to send to Triermain, "for if there is a blanket whole in the place, or more than a rag to sleep the bairns, I am a right goose. And while I think on't, we lack two or three cleanly maids about this house, fie! 'tis like a tavern at Christmas, and those draggles ye have can keep to the scullery, tallow-urchins! It were best ye send to Carlisle for some decent town girls, if such they have. Aye, and for a bed, too, the best down, for I'll sleep in the strappado ere I trust again to that mouldy coffin abovestairs. Well, about it, man, stand not till ye put down roots! Go, go, shuffle and skip!"

She took the cup that Susan brought and drank deep, standing wide-legged before the fire like a captain at an inn, and when I made bold to address her, begging her pardon that it might not wait, stayed me with a finger, and asked Master Lightfoot, who attended upon her, was

not that the Land Sergeant Carleton she had seen ride
away as she came in from Triermain? He saying it was,
she asked not what he had come for, but tapped her lip
and bade him send word to Gilsland bidding him to
dinner the next day, at two o'clock. This being much to
the lawyer's liking, she asked of Lord Scroop, the Warden, were it best she should await him, being new come
to the country, or should she send to him in Carlisle,
and he pondering this with much gravity, bade him consider well and turned to me at last, asking what it was
that would not wait, and tossed her cup to Susan to be
filled.

What with being put off while she talked of light matters, and Lightfoot being there, I was a moment aback,
thinking what I must say.

"Come, sir," says she, "what will not wait is waiting,
and I am waiting, too."

"Oh, madam!" I said, "what the boy told you is true!
The man who served you, Noble the Waitabout, is in
peril of his life!"

"Save us, is that your news?" says she. "When was
he not, from what I've seen of him?"

I cried that this was instant peril, and came of what
he had done at Triermain, "and for this the Land Sergeant will have him slain, oh, not by law, but out of
hand, as it were murdering him, and this to satisfy the
robbers of Liddesdale, lest they take revenge!"

I looked to see her change countenance at this, but
she frowned only and said how should this be, "for did
not the fellow Waitabout tell me they would dare nothing
against us here?"

I said Master Carleton feared that for spite they would
foray elsewhere than here, making excuse to ride on Eng-

land for what was done on English ground, "but, oh, my lady, whatever of that, the Land Sergeant has set on the watch riders to take him in the waste, which they will surely do, and the Deputy Yarrow will send up his head for a token into Scotland!"

Still she changed not her countenance, but taking her cup again from the maid, sipped at it, and then looking to Lightfoot, who stood by scratching his beard in dismay, asked if it was so. He said it was, and watched her shrewdly beneath his brows, but said no more.

"So Master Carleton will throw him to the wolves," says she. "A pretty country!" And asked Susan did this draught come from the small cask they had brought or the great one.

Now at this I cried out aloud, not willing to believe what I saw and heard, that she could stand unmoved and talk lightly of wine, she that had looked with such knowing on the man but three hours since, and vowed her honour to uphold him, and vowed him more than that in her heart. Hearing me cry out she asked what ailed me. In such agony of spirit as I was, I stammered would she not save him?

"What would you have me do?" she asked me, with a pretty little perplexity of her brows, but for her face it was as tranquil as though she were on sleep.

I begged her if she would but write a line and send it after Yarrow, bidding him stay his hand and deliver to her the Waitabout, who was her bound man for any offence done, he would not dare deny her, "and oh, my lady, there is time, if ye but haste, for your boy Peterkin will ride light, and they are in harness, and the smoke on Black Rigg a certain guide! In God's name, my lady!" And seeing her still unmoved I fell on my knees before her.

Master Lightfoot would have spoke, but she checked him, and asked where was this Black Rigg? He knew not, but Hodgson being come in again told her it lay three leagues and more to the south.

"Then he is beyond my charge," said she. "Sit in your chair, Father Lewis, you are not well."

But I must cry on in my despair, entreating her for sweet compassion's sake to do it, as she herself would hope for intercession, "for it is no matter of charges, here or there, or law or any other thing, but only that he took your hand and served you, and you swore to maintain him, and in all conscience, lady, this is the time, God knoweth, and his life hangs on it!"

Hodgson helped me to the chair again, whispering that I should give over a God's name, and when I lifted up my head he was gone and the lawyer withdrawn to the window, but my lady still before the fire who ran her finger about the rim of her cup, then looking on me spake softly out of that fair young face cold as stone.

"I told you yesterday ye should not preach at me, nor shall you read me my conscience neither, for that was done this day by one that knows his world better than you. He served me, aye, and more than he guessed in instruction, and God knows I would have served him, but he willed it not. Mark that, priest, he willed it not! So let him look to himself, for he is not in my charge."

It was like a knell in mine ears, yet I implored her for her own sake not forsake him, lest she repent it most bitterly thereafter. She answered, not one whit, and drank her wine.

Now at such cruel neglect my wrath rose to see those white fingers toy with a cup that would not stir one to save him, and recking nothing I denounced her that hardened her heart out of pride. Then for a moment was she moved indeed, but to anger, for I saw her ill smile come and go fleeting ere she answered softly cold as before.

"Nay, little priest, ye do me wrong, great wrong, yet I mark it not. I do but follow the custom of the country, of which so many have been busy to instruct me, aye, and wisely too, for sure this is not Hampshire but the Scottish frontier, where we must all shift as best we can, and each mind what is within his own charge. Yours, when you are mended, I think should be at Triermain, where you may comfort such silly souls as be of your persuasion. Name them not to me, but shrive 'em heartily as befits your own conscience, and be content with that."

Now I might not speak for a while for grief and bitterness, but she biding by the fire and stirring a fallen log with her foot what time she drained her cup, I said presently that I had no stomach to go again to Triermain that was of evil memory, nor to other of the places about where I had been wont to go, but when my hurts were healed would by her good leave take me away out of that country where I was too soul sick to stay longer.

She gave a light lift of her shoulder and said it should be as I chose, but whither would I go, and when I said I knew not, but would fare as I had told her before wheresoever it pleased God to guide me, said on her dry note that for my soul such faring might be well enough "but for your body 'twere best ye had some good lordship, and though ye make somewhat free to rummage in my conscience and have a nose to more than should concern you, yet God knows ye deserve well of me, that have served me, aye, without bond or bargain, to your own grievous hurt of flesh and, I think, of spirit."

I said, in all humility and gratitude, that she was no

ways obliged to me, and was bidden hold my tongue, "for if it is my pleasure to do you good, you shall take it. For whatever is in your mind, I am not one that forgets my friends or those that serve me, so they have a kindness for me. For good or ill, I pay my scores."

She said she would consider further, but having in her gifts many livings, "among them should be some nook or almshouse where you may bide, so you Pope it not proudly but keep your old heresy in your pocket."

In my weakness I made no remonstrance but thanked her for her goodness to me, yet despising myself that was too weary of spirit to do other. And do still, but live in her almshouse here in the pleasant south, for as she said, and smiled on me as she said it, "Truly I think you were best away, for your own comfort, since this rough country likes you not. For myself I am like to stay awhile, for I am bred of this border." And that, as God sees me, was as true a word as ever she spake.

She now called to her Master Lightfoot, saying she had taken thought and he should send word to my Lord Scroop at Carlisle, bidding him, if it pleased him and his affairs were not too heavy, to dine with her tomorrow, "when we shall have Master Carleton with us and yourself, and we shall look to them for particulars how the world waggeth hereabouts, and take advice as sitting at their feet to be informed, such as where shall I find me a brisk captain to raise a company of horse for protection, and other things. Something o' the Yarrow mould, yet not he who is but a rude callant, but a seasoned fellow, aye, and if he is a reiver it is no matter, so he is not one that hath been to school."

Master Lightfoot inquired should he bid also Lady Scroop, but at this she put out her lip and said no, "for

I mind her at court, a light silly woman, Philadelphia, a great gamester, I'll none of her till I must. Oh, in time you shall list me all the chief gentlemen and their ladies, and from the Scotch side too, and I doubt not we shall give them entertainment enough and be merry, but this while I am for business, and bid no ladies till I know my way among the men."

When he was gone about this business she stood awhile, but looked not on me, and I saw that her thoughts were otherwhere, and to her liking, for she smiled. Then called Susan to take away her cup, and went where the boy Wattie lay on his couch, as he had lain this quarter hour great-eyed and fearful for what he had heard. And indeed I think was in terror to be noticed by her again, and would have risen but she stayed him, asking how he did. He said, well, but for fear of her said no more. She told him pleasantly that it was in her mind there was a little stream not far away, where she had played for minnows when she was a child, and how was it called. He told her, the Ghyll Beck, and she laughed and said she remembered to have fallen in, and he had brought her home all wet and forlorn and that was the time of the sugar plums and dandelion drink.

The clown licked his lips but durst not look on her, saying it was so indeed, and she smiling said that when his wound was healed he should show it her again, "but we'll let the baggies alone, for I've no mind to a ducking these days."

Then left us, he on his couch and myself by the fire, and I heard her sing hey-derry-derry and call for her maid as she ran up the stair.

Historical postscript

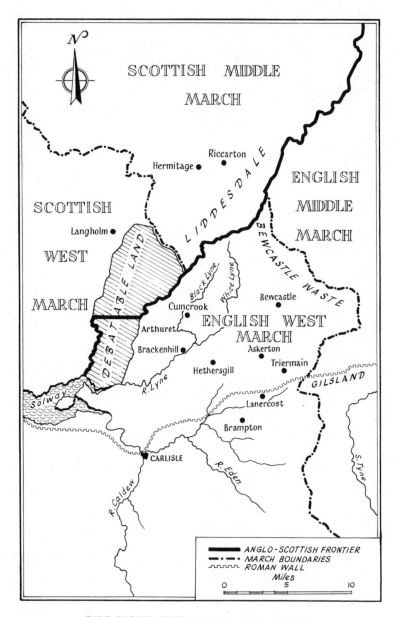

THE WEST BORDER IN THE 1590S.

HISTORICAL POSTSCRIPT

Their [the Grahams'] friends first spoiled 4 of Mistris
Dacres tenants, fired 2 of her towns and 2 of Her
Majesty's, carried off 400 nolte in a day foray, and
lye quiet never a night.

THOMAS, LORD SCROPE,
English West March Warden, to Lord Burghley,
Secretary of State, July 15, 1596

Nicksouns, and other Scots, 30 in all, ran a day foray
in Gilsland, took 40 kie and oxen, and spoiled the
houses of the Bells my cosen Dacre's tenants.

Scrope to Burghley, April 2, 1597

THESE TWO BRIEF EXTRACTS from Scrope's correspondence started the train of thought which took me along *The
Candlemass Road*. The raids they describe were commonplace
enough affairs by border standards – for once, no one was
killed, the "towns" would be no more than villages, the 400
stolen cattle would certainly not be an underestimate – and it
is clear from the contexts that the harassed Warden regarded
them as incidents of no special importance; he merely men-
tions them in passing before returning to weightier matters.
They caught my attention – or rather, my fancy – only because
the victims were both members of the once-great Dacre
family, and one of them was evidently a woman of some
consequence.

To put the two raids in perspective, and to give some idea
of the chaotic state of the Anglo-Scottish frontier at that time,
I should explain that the first extract occurs in the middle of
one of Scrope's impassioned tirades about the wickedness of
the Grahams. Burghley probably sighed when he read it, for
he knew the obsession, amounting almost to mania, which

Scrope had developed about that incorrigible tribe of Border rustlers. They were really no worse than any of the other robber families whose feuds and forays kept the border in continual bloody turmoil, but they were especially odious to Scrope because, unlike the Scottish reivers against whom he waged an endless and futile campaign, they were fellow-Englishmen; not only that, they were Englishmen who had brought the business of aiding and abetting Scottish raids to a fine art. Only lately they had assisted in the dramatic rescue of the notorious Kinmont Willie Armstrong from Carlisle Castle, Scrope's own headquarters, an exploit equivalent to modern terrorists snatching a prisoner from a maximum security jail. It had been the great scandal of 1596, causing an international furore, driving Queen Elizabeth into a storm of oaths and correspondence, encouraging the border thieves to more mischief than ever, and making the unlucky Warden the laughing-stock of the frontier.

The poor man's only relief was to pour out his troubles to Burghley, which he did at length for several months, pleading to be relieved of his office, damning Scott of Buccleuch who had led the rescue (and he a law officer, too, as Scrope never tired of pointing out), complaining of the "awfulness" of the Grahams and the "soft usage" they were receiving, despite Scrope's protests, from the London government, and despairing of ever doing anything with them – his July 15 letter noted moodily that he had "hanged fyve or six" of them, but it would probably only make the rest of the family worse.

As a specimen of the reports that Wardens wrote to their governments in that grim decade when the frontier was sinking to new depths of lawlessness and barbarism, it is fairly typical, although Scrope had a richer vocabulary of indignation than most, and a fine line in self-pity. We should feel sorry for him; he was a brave and busy law officer trying to do an impossible job with three strikes against him from the start: he was of that devious nature which mistrusts everyone, he was the son and successor of one of the most respected Wardens in border history whose boots he was not competent to fill, and he seems to have been constitutionally unlucky, not only in his work. Like his wife, Philadelphia, he was a compulsive gambler and consequently in debt (he once tried to touch Burghley's son, Robert Cecil, for £300, apparently without success).

One unusual feature of his July 15 letter is that for once he does not punctuate his vilification of the Grahams with abuse of his other great *bête noire* – Thomas Carleton, his former deputy and Constable of the Castle, now demoted by Scrope and employing his talents for intrigue and general mischief in the minor office of Land Sergeant of Gilsland. Carleton, the Warden suspected (with reason), was now deliberately encouraging Scottish inroads, using his position to pay off old scores, conspiring with the Grahams to spite Scrope, and had been a prime mover in the Kinmont affair, along with his insolent and reckless younger brother, Lance – a nice example of border officers hand-in-glove with their country's enemies, to the discomfiture of their superior. Normally the Carletons' iniquities, real or imagined, were good for several tooth-grinding passages in Scrope's letters, but this time Burghley was spared.

That is the background to his July 15 blast against the Grahams, which would not have awoken my interest (like Burghley, I had heard it all before) but for its passing reference to the recent raid and fire-raising on "Mistris Dacres" land. It is the kind of thing that Wardens frequently dropped into their reports, not as any special outrage, but just to remind London of what they were up against. And if Scrope singled this one out from all the murders, forays, burnings, and extortions that took place daily and nightly in his march, we may be sure it was for no better reason than that the despoilers were "friends" of the Grahams; here was another stick, if not a very stout one, to beat them with, and had he not been able to drag them in, it is unlikely that we would ever have heard of the unfortunate lady and her burned-out tenants. Scrope makes no definite reference to her in his later correspondence, and I have found no bill "fouled"* against reivers who can be positively identified as the raiders, or any suggestion that she ever received redress under the erratic border law.

Which is not necessarily a reproach to Scrope. Like every Warden, he was in the position of today's inner city police, struggling to keep the peace against the odds, and lucky if he could cope with one outrage in ten. He simply had too much to do, what with his prime duty of negotiating and temporising with his opposite numbers on the Scotch side (who included such mavericks as Buccleuch and Robert "Fyrebrande" Kerr, who were lawmen or lawbreakers as they felt inclined), dealing with the "knaveries and accustomed devilish devises" of the Grahams and those "spoylers and outlaws" the Carletons, vainly trying to stir London into action, and running Warden forays (official reprisal raids) against the likes of Kinmont Willie. For all the time he gave to his voluminous correspondence with Burghley, "the keen Lord Scroop"† probably spent more hours in the saddle than at his desk.

So it is not surprising that the Dacre raid received only brief notice in passing, and perhaps nothing illustrates more starkly the deplorable condition of the marches than that almost casual reference, in the middle of a bitter general harangue by a tired and despondent official, to four settlements burned, tenants harried, and 400 cattle stolen – it is something by the way, a piece of the small change of border life. As I said at the beginning, a commonplace which caught my eye only because the victim was a woman of some importance.

Women do not figure largely in the annals of border reiving, and when they do they tend to be either aristocrats or formidable – like the kidnapped Countess of Northumberland, or old Lady Forster shooting the bolt in the nick of time as assassins

---

* A bill "fouled" or "fyled" was a case proved at a truce day meeting where the Wardens of both sides heard complaints and gave redress.

† "Scrope" is the usual spelling, but Border writers frequently rendered it as Scroop.

stormed up the stairs to her husband's bedchamber, or the goodwife who bargained for her husband's life in a frontier skirmish, or the anonymous Amazon in the old ballad "The Fray of Suport", rallying her riders to hot trod after she had been raided ("Fie, lads, my gear's a' gane!") She came to mind when my eye fell on "Mistris Dacre" because their plights seemed to be identical, and I found myself wondering what, if anything, the latter had done to answer the burning of her "towns" and the spoiling of her people, since the law apparently could do nothing.

That was the germ of *The Candlemass Road*; the second quoted extract confirmed that the leading character should be a raided Dacre, and supplied identities for the spoilers and the immediate victims. It comes from a letter written by Scrope nine months later, when conditions should have been more settled: a commission was meeting to consider border affairs, the King of Scotland was at Dumfries, and the mercurial Buccleuch was peacefully engaged in organising "a special horse race" in Liddesdale to be attended by "nobilitie, officers, and subjects" – none of which soothed the Warden's paranoia. He knew what race meetings could lead to; like football matches they were all too often convenient covers for conspiracy, and he reminded Burghley on a rising note that the last race meeting Buccleuch had attended had been the assembly point for the Kinmont raiders. Now, as then, the Grahams were being "familiar" with Buccleuch, and "I praye God, Buclughe doth not with this rase as he did this tyme twelve monethes" – Scrope's spelling, erratic even by Elizabethan standards, deteriorated with agitation. He was taking no chances, he told Burghley; his riders were on an hour's warning, for to add to his anxieties Liddesdale raiders had been plundering in England even while the commission was sitting – and at this point in the letter comes the quoted reference to the Nixons' foray against "the Bells my cosen Dacre's tenants". Again, as in the case of the raid mentioned in his earlier letter, Scrope plainly considers this foray a minor affair; he refers to it only to give the lie to his enemy Lance Carleton, who had been putting it about that the English Bells were in league with the Liddesdale reivers.

However, I was not concerned with my Lord Scrope's problems, which I had researched and written about years earlier;* what interested me, idly enough at first, were the questions raised by those two raids, and the possible answers. Could "Mistris Dacre" also be Scrope's "cosen Dacre"? What kin was she to the famous Lord Thomas Dacre who eighty years before had been the terror of English and Scottish reivers alike – or to Leonard "Crookback" Dacre the arch-rebel of only twenty years before? Had the Liddesdale robbers singled her out as a specially tempting target, and if so why? Could feud be involved, or blackmail, or reprisal? Did the raid have any connection with the complex Carleton-Bell vendetta which was taking place that same springtime?

If I had felt inclined to venture again into the confusion of border records I might have found the answers to these and other questions, but I doubt it. The two incidents are small knots in a great tangled web, and I knew enough of the crazy pattern of West March politics, with its criss-crossing threads of raid, feud, kinship, alliance, double-dealing, and misinformation, woven by so many untrustworthy hands, to realise that I was unlikely to succeed where my lords Burghley and Scrope had so often had to admit failure.

And there was no need to try, since what I was contemplating was not the writing of more border history, but of a fiction based firmly on border fact which might convey something that a straight history could not. In my mind was a lesson that every historical novelist learns with his first researches – that no work of history written at a distance can ever give as vivid and informative a picture as a contemporary writer, be he journalist, diarist, or novelist. (Sometimes I think the novelists do it best, and not only the giants. Surtees and Thomas Hughes catch the feel and authentic image of their time just as surely as Dickens does; no modern historian that

* *The Steel Bonnets, The Story of the Anglo-Scottish Border Reivers* (Harvill)

I know has evoked the atmosphere of '30s London as well as James Curtis and Leslie Charteris, or, for the austerity years after the war, Hadley Chase. And if I want to recapture California, I go to Raymond Chandler and Budd Schulberg.)

I was well aware that in writing border history I had failed entirely to catch the borderers in close-up. One can give the facts, the names, the explanations, but the people as they were and moved and talked and lived, is another story. Unfortunately, no Elizabethan had written it; Wardens and other reporters were concerned with official matters; when they touched on human detail, it was for a fleeting moment only. (If only Thomas Dekker had visited the border; the Reiver's Hornbook would have been a treasure beyond price.) One writer alone had given more than a glimpse: Robin Carey, the sprightly young adventurer-courtier-lawman whose tantalisingly brief *Memoirs* are the nearest thing we have to a living picture of the reiver's frontier. With him we see ambush at first hand, and play tig with the riding families in the wilderness, and lie out in the mosses, waiting, and learn how to attack a peel tower (Thomas Carleton showed him, on the spot), and through him, just once, we actually hear a reiver talking: Geordie Burn, Scotch thief of Teviotdale, reviewing his disgraceful life on the night before his hanging, with the disguised Carey taking notes.

My effort could only be a poor tenth-best, but I might come at least a little closer to catching the people and their frontier with a "contemporary fiction" than I had done with a history. It must contain nothing by way of incident, character, language, and detail that did not have warranty in the letters and reports of Wardens, envoys, travellers, churchmen, spies, and the rest, and, for what it was worth, there would be my own knowledge of the reivers' descendants, among whom I had been born, raised, educated, married, worked, played rugby, and gone to war – for "outman, Scotsman, and forroner" or not, I too was bred of that border.

Characters and plot were suggested by the Scrope extracts: "Mistris Dacre", the often-harried Bells her tenants, the Nixon raiders, and the absence of official protection and redress. To these I added what I knew of blackmail levied, paid, and occasionally resisted; of feud and reprisal; of the lengths to which the riding folk would go to repay debt or injury; of the "unblessed hand"; of the broken men; of the arbitrary power of lordship; of that bond which bound the land and people into something beyond the ken of elsewhere England and Scotland; of the reivers and their methods, customs, weapons, and strange code of honour; of the tortuous policy of officers like Carleton labouring, under the conflicting pressures of nationality, friendship, fear, and safety, to reconcile their interest with their duty; of the condition of the common folk who were "every man's prey"; and of the wind and rain off the fells.

Since some of the characters I have used were real, and the rest are so well represented in the Border Papers that I can hardly call them creatures of my imagination, I should say something about them and their background.

The Dacres were once the leading family of Cumberland, but by the closing years of the sixteenth century their great days were over. They were never a "riding surname" (robber tribe) like the Armstrongs, Charltons, Elliots, Grahams, and others; their leaders were too genteel for that sort of thing, although they were always to the fore in border wars and reprisal raids. At their peak they were Wardens, sheriffs, and Governors of Carlisle, the most famous being the reckless and belligerent Lord Thomas Dacre, who was my model for old Lord Ralph; the only liberty was in shifting him from the first half of the century to the second.

Tom Dacre was a brilliant soldier and a wild man; as a youth he had risked his life by carrying off and marrying a seventeen-year-old beauty, Elizabeth Greystoke, in defiance of her guardian, Lord Clifford, and went on to win a great name as border fighter and warlord – "there is noo herdyer nor bettir knyght, but often time he doth not use the most sure order," wrote Surrey the victor of Flodden, where Thomas Dacre led the Cumbrian riders and was the first man to reach the Scottish king, a former friend whom he had been in the habit of fleecing at cards. As Warden, Thomas held the West March against all comers, Scots and English, for sixteen years, and at an advanced age was still laying about him on foot at the battle of Jedburgh, despite "the gowte" which forced his retirement soon afterwards. Unlike my Lord Ralph (whose murder I based on that of the Scots Warden Carmichael), Thomas "the old red bull" died of a fall from his horse. He left behind him the Askerton stronghold which he had built in North Cumberland, and a memorable quotation which summed up his philosophy: "There was never so mekill myschefe, robbry, spoiling and vengeance in Scotland then there is nowe . . . which I praye our Lord God to continewe."

His son later held the Wardenship, but was not a success, and the power of the family finally declined when their estates and title passed to the Howards through the marriage of Thomas's grand-daughter Elizabeth. Her uncle, the rightful heir, was the "cankred, suttil traitor" Leonard Dacre, known as Crookback, a splendid villain who tried to regain the inheritance by joining and then betraying the rebellion of the "bankrupt earls" of Northumberland and Westmoreland, who hoped to release Mary Queen of Scots, then imprisoned at Tutbury in the Midlands. The revolt (during which Northumberland's Countess fell into the hands of the Liddesdale reivers, from whom she was rescued by the Kerrs) petered out, and Leonard, who had gathered a force of three thousand English and Scottish reivers and outlaws and briefly regained two of the family's castles, was badly beaten by Warden forces at the battle on Gelt River in 1570, from which he was the first to flee, en route to Scotland and the Continent, leaving the Dacres' famous red bull standard in the grasp of Hunsdon, the victorious Warden.

After which, border records contain only echoes of the family's great days, but more of raid and distress suffered, of a claim by the Lowthers on Dacre land, of Dacre tenants paying blackmail to the notorious Richie Graham, of threats

167

from Liddesdale, of a Dacre suspected of harbouring Jesuits, and most significant of all, a letter of 1601 referring to the family's 300-year feud with the Musgraves, which contains the phrase: "For the Dacres: if ever in theire greatness (or since) . . ."

So were the mighty fallen, and the last mention of the once-feared war cry is in a report of March 20, 1601, describing how Kinmont Willie and others, including "Inglish disobedientes", apparently on a drunken spree, "brack and cutt upp the postes" of Carlisle's north gate, "cutt upp their doores, toke prisoners &c", and rode below the city walls roaring "Upon them, upon theym, a Daker, a Daker, a read bull, a read bull".

It is somewhere late in that period of gradual decline that I have placed the fictional Lady Margaret,* inspired by "Mistris Dacre" but closer, in imagination, to those noblewomen of the great Northern families who, tied by blood and birth to the frontier, often grew up in the gentler airs of the south – like old Thomas's three grand-daughters, Anne, Mary and Elizabeth ("Bessie wi' the braid apron") through whom the Dacre inheritance passed by marriages with Philip Howard of Arundel and Lord William ("Bauld Willie") Howard – there is a fine homeliness about Northern nicknames. Another vague inspiration was that lively "Lady of Gilsland", Elizabeth Greystoke, who bewitched old Thomas into playing Lochinvar. But my Lady Margaret's character is all her own.

The broken man who champions her may seem an unusual figure – educated reivers given to free thinking are thin on the

---

* I installed her at Askerton because it seemed the obvious residence for her, as did Triermain for her tenants; both places were geographically suitable, and had Dacre associations, although in fact Askerton had passed to the Crown following Leonard Crookback's treason, and towards the end of the sixteenth century was one of the "fees" of the Land Sergeants of Gilsland – one of whom, ironically, was "Thomas Carleton, gentleman". See the Muster of Gilsland, September 5, 1598, taken by his successor, John Musgrave, (Calendar of Border Papers, ii, 990) and the Certificate of Gilsland Barony from Mr Auditor King (August 16, 1598, C.B.P., ii, 982).

ground in the Border Papers – but he is easily accounted for by his association with the remarkable teacher whom he calls "the gallows priest", that rugged saint Bernard Gilpin of Tynedale (1517–83), rector of Houghton-le-Spring, whose pastoral work among the robber families of Redesdale and Tynedale can only be called heroic. Gilpin was a Westmorland man and fellow of Queen's College, Oxford, whose reforming views and condemnation of clerical abuses led to his denunciation as a heretic during Queen Mary's reign, but a broken leg delayed his being taken south to probable martyrdom and in the meantime the Queen died, leaving the "Apostle of the North" to continue his eccentric ministry under Elizabeth.

By all accounts he was a robust and fearless preacher, but it was his hardihood, courage, and simple kindness which endeared him to the riding families on his annual winter pilgrimages into the heart of reiver country; he would give his clothes to a beggar, his horse to a distressed peasant, and the freedom of his table to all comers every Sunday; many of the boys who attended his grammar school (and some went on to make their names at the great universities) were fed and lodged at his expense. He was raided and plundered during the rising of the "bankrupt earls" – and strove manfully to save rebel riders from the gallows when the revolt was crushed. The Bishopric of Carlisle and the provostship of his old college were offered to him, but he chose to stay with his lawless charges, and when he died – ironically, the reivers' priest was knocked down by an ox in Durham market – he left a name honoured for many generations in the borderland. From him, I choose to think, the wandered waif Archie Noble learned his Latin and much more besides.

The Waitabout character owes his surname, birth, and perhaps some of his personality to a shadowy figure of border legend who may possibly be identified with a real person in border history – Hobbie Noble, who occurs in two of the better-known ballads, one of which describes him as:

                              an English man,
          In Bewcastle-dale was bred and born,
          But his misdeeds they were sae great,
          They banished him neer to return.

Some versions have him banished "to Liddisdale", but in
all versions he is an English reiver riding with the Armstrongs.
In the ballad "Jock o' the Side", Hobbie leads the rescue
of Jock from Newcastle jail; in "Hobie Noble" he guides an
Armstrong raid into Cumberland, is betrayed by his leading
accomplice, Sim Armstrong of the Mains, to the Land Sergeant at Askerton, who takes him captive to Carlisle, where
he is offered his life if he will confess to horse-stealing, refuses,
and is hanged.

The heroes and villains of border ballads are bluntly drawn,
as a rule, without much finesse, but the figure of Hobbie (Hal-
bert or Albert) Noble has some unusual characteristics: in one
version he is something of a wit, and is described as smiling
(which is rare in ballads); he is also a man of principle, loyal,
fearless, and cool in crisis, and there is evident respect for
"brave Noble" from his enemies. Child, the most scholarly of
ballad authorities, finds him a gallant figure who "will always
command the hearty liking of those who live too late to suffer
from [his misdeeds]".

But in stating that the ballads are all we know of this genial
reiver, Child may have been mistaken. There was a "Hobbe
Noble" living and reiving in Bewcastle in 1583, according to
the list of "riders and ill-doers" drawn up for Burghley by
Thomas Musgrave, Captain of Bewcastle. He names this
"Hobbe Noble" first among twenty-three "Nobles, Taylors,
some of the Grames, and a few Storyes living next to the
Nixons of the Black and White Lyne rivers", and "hard
by the house [fort] of Bewcastell" where Musgrave had his
own head-quarters. Bewcastle, a wasteland at the eastern
end of the English West March, was a haunt of outlaws and
broken men, and was constantly being crossed by raiders,
especially the Scots forayers of Liddesdale which lay only

five miles away. (Musgrave, although a law officer, was as great a rascal as any of his reiving neighbours but can be relied on for factual information of this kind; indeed, he is the leading authority.)

A few weeks after Musgrave's list was drawn up, Henry Scrope, West March Warden and father of the unlucky Thomas, wrote as follows to Sir Francis Walsingham:

"Hobbe of Cumcrooke is an English outlaw resett [harboured] sometimes in both countries – for whose apprehension I shall do my diligence."

One has to be wary of jumping to tempting conclusions, but I should be surprised if "Hobbe Noble" of the list and "Hobbe of Cumcrooke" were not one and the same. Cumcrook lies only four miles from Bewcastle Fort, close to the Black Lyne, and Musgrave notes only one other "Hobbe" in the entire area, a Nixon of no apparent importance called "Malles Hobbe". Given that Scrope singled out "Hobbe of Cumcrooke" for special attention, and that Musgrave gives "Hobbe Noble" priority in a sizeable gang of Bewcastle villains, the assumption of common identity seems not too unreasonable; it is also interesting that the scant details given about "Hobbe of Cumcrooke" fit exactly with the Hobbie Noble of the ballads – English, outlaw, a foot in both realms. Consider, too, that those ballads contain the names of three other reivers who were living men in this generation – Jock of the Side, Sim of the Mains, and Laird's Jock Armstrong – and there is at least circumstantial evidence for identifying the Hobbie of the ballads with both Musgrave's Hobbe and Scrope's Hobbe.

But whether as Bewcastle outlaw of history or as the articulate, jesting, expert frontiersman of legend, Hobbie Noble served as a model for Archie Waitabout, whom I envisaged as a reiver's child orphaned and cast adrift after some foray, finding his way, as so many border lads did, to the care of Bernard Gilpin in nearby Tynedale, and no doubt trying that good man's patience for several years before his wild nature took him back to the hills and mosses in young manhood. There he might well serve as a Warden trooper in the earls' rebellion, and as a Johnstone rider in the great slaughter of the Maxwells at Dryfe Sands, shifting from one allegiance to another before becoming a footloose march wanderer and broken man on the edge of outlawry. The Nixons he fought on Lady Margaret's behalf might be his old comrades; certainly they would be kin to those Lyne River Nixons who had been his childhood neighbours and probable relations. This was the way of the border, and the despair of Wardens and governments – that sworn friends one year could be bitter enemies the next, that feuds could run in circles (Armstrong against Robson against Elliot against Scott against Kerr against Turnbull against . . . Armstrong again), that some families were both Scottish and English, that others would change their national allegiance overnight (or, in battle, at a moment's notice), and that in all things the borderer was a law (for want of a better word) unto himself.

One other historical figure lent something to Archie Waitabout and he was a "notorious felon at large", Jock Graham of the Peartree. Awaiting trial for horse-theft at Carlisle, he was broken out of the city by his brother Wattie, and later, when Wattie in his turn was taken and due to hang at Appleby, Jock repaid the favour with some ingenuity. Wattie had been arrested by Sheriff Salkeld, so Jock kidnapped the Sheriff's six-year-old son, and used him as a hostage for his brother's release. Ruthlessness born of necessity, certainly, but at least it was done with some style: Jock rode alone and by day, regardless of risk, to Salkeld's country house, found the little boy playing by the gate, and offered him an apple with the invitation: "Master, will you ride?" Little Salkeld accepted, and was spirited away – and was returned safe and sound when Wattie was set free. Jock of the Peartree's eventual fate is uncertain; a few years later, when the authorities were sweeping the riding families from the frontier after the Union of the Crowns, he was in the Low Countries (probably serving as a mercenary, as many reivers did, upon compulsion) but returned and was arrested in London. He may have been transported to Ulster with the rest of the Grahams in the early 1600s.

Which brings me to the one entirely real major character in the story, Thomas Carleton. The Land Sergeant receives extensive coverage in border letters and reports, and I have presented him as faithfully as I can. Even allowing for the poisonous hatred that colours Thomas Scrope's descriptions of him and his swaggering younger brother, he does seem to have been, if not a complete scoundrel, at least a most subtle, devious, and untrustworthy operator. He was also intelligent, patient, brave, and a first-class law officer when it suited him and he had no ulterior purpose to serve.

I confess to some sympathy for him; his was an impossible duty, on such a frontier, where national and local politics had to be conducted in a confusion of crime and feud and contrary loyalties, and only a rigidly upright outsider, untrammelled by border ties, could hope to steer a straight course. Thomas Carleton was practically horizontal, and a borderer to his backbone, but while he was frequently deep in knavery, and ever ready to resort to deceit and betrayal – just now and then we have a sense of a clever, worldly and probably weary man doing his best, or at least not his worst. He spent a dangerous lifetime in negotiating and dealing and making do, and when all else failed, fighting it out whatever the odds.

His duty, and his courage, cost him his life in the end. A Scots prisoner in his charge, David Elliot, had killed one of the English Ogles in feud; the Ogles, thirteen strong, took advantage of Carleton's absence to ride to the house where Elliot was held, and murdered him, taking care to injure no one else. Knowing Carleton's many "understandings" with the Scottish thieves, it is quite possible that he had been sheltering Elliot rather than holding him prisoner; in the event he "voud to have the lives" of the Ogles and ran them down with a posse of six riders. The Ogles tried to reason with him, but he came raging at them with lance and pistol, unhorsing one

173

of them. In desperation the Ogles opened fire and that was the end of Thomas Carleton, "the expert borderer".

What happened to his brother Lance is a mystery; he was last heard of in 1602, writing to the government offering to murder the Earl of Tyrone. Since Tyrone survived until 1616, we may assume that the offer was not accepted.

Other real borderers of the time appear briefly or are mentioned in the story: the murderous Willie Kang Irvine, the "great thief" John Charlton of the Bower, Hutcheon Graham, Auld Wat of Harden, and various Wardens – the Carey brothers, Robin and John, and their tempestuous father, Hunsdon, widely believed to be a bastard son of Henry VIII. Thomas "the Merchant" Hetherington, one of that refractory English tribe who descended on Carlisle in 1569 intending to murder the Bishop, was a blackmailer and associate of Richie Graham, a colourful ruffian who in addition to his protection racket also ran a counterfeiting business in his tower at Brackenhill, a few miles from Carlisle. Since many of "the Merchant's" blackmail clients were Hetheringtons, I suspect some ingenious family ploy was being worked; Richie Graham may have reached the same conclusion, for we read of him "denying" Thomas Hetherington shortly after. Those tenants who would not pay, incidentally, were raided and plundered by Richie's Scottish nephews, and when one of the victims appealed for help to Thomas Carleton ("then in company of said Richard Grame") the Land Sergeant "replied that he could do him no good". No wonder young Scrope despaired.

The Nixon raiders were in fact as I have described them in fiction. The tribe was a bi-national one, living in scattered pockets in both West Marches, but the main branch of the Scottish Nixons formed an unholy quadruple alliance with the Armstrongs, Elliots, and Crosers (Croziers) of Liddesdale which was the scourge of the frontier – indeed, I doubt if, in British history, including that of the Highlands, there is to be found such a reign of crime and terror as those four families inflicted on their neighbours from the Middle Ages to the end of the sixteenth century. The list of bills "fouled" against them is an appalling one, and it can have been only a fraction of their raids, murders, burnings, extortions, and kidnappings; they were the worst of a bad border, and all the more fearsome for their concentration in numbers in one valley: at their strongest they could put more than two thousand lances in the saddle in time of war, or in the great sweeps through the northern counties in which whole townships and tracts of countryside were despoiled. Raids in hundreds were more common, and forays by small family gangs of anything from six to twenty riders most common of all. And they were not the romantic outlaws of minstrelsy and folklore, but ruthless pillagers and killers who survived centuries of war and reprisal and large-scale punitive expeditions by both governments, which devastated their valley without dislodging them.

"Ill Will" and "Fingerless Will" were reivers of the early 1500s; Clemmie "the Clash" Nixon and "Half-drowned Geordie" Nixon were raiding Gilsland in October, 1595. "Hungry Jock" is based on Geordie Burn, mentioned earlier.

The Bells, once "a great surname", were to be found in both West Marches. They had solid credentials in raid and feud, but by the end of the century had become less aggressive, although individuals like Willie "Redcloak" Bell and his brothers, who had taken part in the Kinmont rescue, and Christopher Bell, outlaw and hired assassin, did their best to keep the family's bad name alive. The Triermain Bells of my story are loosely based on the Bells of Gilsland, a contentious and (by their own account) much injured community; they do seem to have endured more than their share of raiding and blackmailing in the '90s, when we find them complaining of their wrongs to the Privy Council, thanking the Wardens for the liberation of 100 of their number kidnapped in one day foray by Scots riders, protesting their respectability and loyalty, and warning that unless protection is forthcoming they expect to be "cleane rooted out of those parts".

A moving tale, until we look further in the papers for 1596–7, and find these same Gilsland Bells charged with plotting the assassination of Thomas Carleton "and all his kin" because he had delivered Christopher Bell to execution for *eleven* murders; they had also procured the hanging of two Carleton adherents by false witness, were at feud with the Grahams, and were alleged also to be feuding with the Armstrongs and at the same time assisting Armstrong raids into England (by no means impossible). After which it is rather an anticlimax to find them being advised to "mend theyre manners" by Henry Leigh – an active and interesting border officer who was at various times deputy Warden, confidante of James VI, government spy, and fugitive, last mentioned in the records as hiding in a wood in Lancashire in a false beard. Not that that necessarily had anything to do with the Bells, but it may be an instructive sidelight on border affairs.

As to the sins and injuries of the Bells, it depends entirely on which untrustworthy witnesses you believe; there is no doubt that they were heavily raided and blackmailed, and well qualified for the role of victim. There were many George Bells, and I had in mind those "poore and dailye suppliantes . . . utterlye beggered and spoiled" whose lament of November 18, 1597 may have moved the Privy Council, but not Thomas Carleton, who simply called them liars, "which God forgeve them".

Finally, my narrator, Frey Luis Guevara, although he is a fictional character, had his counterparts on the Tudor frontier, where the folk were as likely to be Roman or pagan as Protestant, and many priests of the old faith were to be found, more or less anonymous as prudence and local feeling dictated. His name had no modern inspiration; there were two Guevaras on the border at this time, though they were not priests. John Guevara was a deputy Warden of the East March, with a talent for snatching English fugitives out of Scotland undetected; he seems to have come under a cloud for questionable activities on behalf of his Warden, Lord Willoughby, and his troop command was passed to his brother, Harry Guevara, of whom I know nothing more.

So those were the materials I used to make *The Candlemass Road*, a fiction which is simply an echo of events which happened every day along the border. In that, it is a true story, and its people, noble and simple, reiver and officer, once lived on the Marches, not so long ago. They were indeed a strange folk, terrible and admirable, and anyone who studies them – even if it is just to read through that part of their story which is to be found in the two volumes of the Calendar of Border Papers – will learn much about the matter of Britain, and perhaps feel indebted to them. Whatever their faults, they were realists who learned about life and death the hard way, and had at heart the lesson that when the walls of the ivory tower are broken down, and survival is in the balance, one must shift as best can, according to the custom of the country.

GLOSSARY

a-kenbo	akimbo, hand(s) on hip(s)
amain	forcefully; also, with speed
Anthropophagi	legendary cannibals, not mentioned in "Mandeville", but described by Bernard Gilpin in a sermon before Edward VI in 1552
Babees Booke	fifteenth century children's book on table manners, etc.
baggies	minnows
balladine	comic dancer
bantling	infant, brat
barnekin	wall enclosing ground of peel tower or house
bastel	fortified house or tower
bell (racing)	the usual prize at border race meetings; the Carlisle Bell is said to be the oldest racing trophy in existence. One such bell was run "for my lady Dacre's sake".
billy	close companion, comrade
brangling	heated argument
caliver	light musket
Carel	Carlisle
chestayne	chestnut
cingle	girdle
clarting	smearing with mud, dirtying
Cloudsley, William	a legendary Cumbrian bowman, hero of the ballad "Adam Bell, Clim of the Clough, and William of Cloudislee". He is one of many Northern archers credited with shooting an apple from his son's head.

178

cotch	coach
dag	pistol
Debatable Land	a strip of land, about twelve miles by three, just north of Carlisle at the western extremity of the frontier, and claimed by both countries. It was finally divided between the realms in 1552, but continued to be a notorious nest of outlaws.
Derrick, Thomas	Tyburn hangman (fl. 1600) who gave his name to hoisting equipment.
double and sawfey	a fine commonly imposed on a convicted thief, amounting to three times the value of the stolen goods
fast	secured, stuck
featly	deftly, neatly
fenny goose	marchland goose; dropped feathers were supposedly best for fletching arrows
fyled, fouled	found guilty, case proved
gleek	jibe, jeer, but also to look sidelong or sly
handfasted	engaged to marry; also trial marriage
handsel	well-wishing, welcoming, inauguration
hobby, hobbler	small, nimble border horse
hot trod	lawful pursuit of thieves
hot water	spirits
insight	household goods
jack	leather jacket plated with horn or iron
jealously	closely, vigilantly
Jedburgh axe	a form of poleaxe, a.k.a. a Jedburgh staff
Jeddart justice	execution without trial (from "Jedburgh")
jordan	chamber-pot
kie, kye	cattle
la'l	little
Land Sergeant	officer in charge of barony or district, with duties of guard, pursuit, and arrest
let	prevent, hinder. Archaic term meaning

	precisely the opposite of "let" (allow, permit); it lingers on in tennis.
Lickingstone Cell	a dungeon of Carlisle Castle where the only water available came from a permanently moist stone. The groove licked by generations of prisoners, and the hand-print beside it, can still be seen.
Mandeville, Sir John	reputed author of a celebrated travel book c. 1366. Part of it may be a genuine record of journeys in the Middle East but its fame rests on "Mandeville's" descriptions· of mythical monsters and freaks, including basilisks, the Head Right Hideous, and the one-footed folk.
mind (v.)	remember, bear in mind
October	ale brewed in that month (cf. March ale)
plump watch	a fixed guard, not patrolling
pomaunder	pomander, small case or bag of aromatic herbs
poniard	dagger
potched	poached (cookery)
powdered beef	spiced beef; also pickled, preserved
prime	first hour of day (in Frey Luis's case, 9 a.m.)
privado	comrade
reiver	raider, rustler
russled	wrestled
scaur	scar
skilly	skilful
snell	bitter, biting (of weather)
speer	ask, inquire
stoupe, stoup	tankard
strappado	torture in which victim's arms are dislocated by hoisting and dropping with cords
truce day	frontier meeting at which Wardens of both sides tried complaints before a jury of borderers

vagrom	vagrant
visor	mask
Warden	governor, law-giver, military commander, and guardian of a March, of which there were three (West, Middle, East) on either side of the border